MIDNIGHT IN ROSARY

Borgo Press Books by CHARLES ALLEN GRAMLICH

MIDNIGHT IN ROSARY

TALES OF VAMPIRES AND WEREWOLVES IN CRIMSON AND BLACK

CHARLES ALLEN GRAMLICH

THE BORGO PRESS

MMXI

MIDNIGHT IN ROSARY

FIRST EDITION

Published by Wildside Press LLC

www.wildsidebooks.com

DEDICATION

To Lana,

For everything

CONTENTS

ACKNOWLEDGMENTS

THESE STORIES AND POEMS WERE previously published as follows, and are reprinted (with minor editing, updating, and textual modifications) by permission of the author:

"The Cold of Snow and Ghosts" was first published in *Prisoners of the Night*, 1993. Copyright © 1993, 2011 by Charles Allen Gramlich.

"Wanting the Mouth of a Lover" was first published in *Prisoners of the Night*, 1994. Copyright © 1994, 2011 by Charles Allen Gramlich.

"Vessel for the Holy" was first published in *Prisoners of the Night*, 1997. Copyright © 1997, 2011 by Charles Allen Gramlich.

"Clowns in the Dark" was first published in *Prisoners of the Night*, 1990. Copyright © 1990, 2011 by Charles Allen Gramlich.

"Messiah" was first published in *Dead of Night*, 1990. Copyright © 1990, 2011 by Charles Allen Gramlich.

"Night Fall" was first published in *Dead of Night*, 1994. Copyright © 1994, 2011 by Charles Allen Gramlich.

"What Was Asked; What Was Given" was first published in *Prisoners of the Night*, 1995. Copyright © 1995, 2011 by Charles Allen Gramlich.

"When the White Mist" was first published in *Night to Dawn*, 2007. Copyright © 2007, 2011 by Charles Allen Gramlich.

"Thorn" was first published as "Roses and Thorns" in *Tales on the Twisted Side*, 1989. Copyright © 1989, 2011 by Charles Allen Gramlich.

"The Lady Wore Black" was first published in *Prisoners*

PREFACE

With a few exceptions, this collection features vampires and their close relatives the werewolves. Of course, there are many kinds of vampirism and lycanthropy. Not all involve beings that once were human. The "hunger" and the "beast" are ancient archetypes for our species.

The first vamps I met stalked *'Salem's Lot*. Man, they were cool. Deadly, too, but with a disturbingly seductive and rotted beauty. The next vampire novel that I recall with fondness was Robert McCammon's *They Thirst*, about some of the nastiest bloodsuckers you'd ever want to meet razing Los Angeles in search of gore. Only later did I venture back to the originators, first to Bram Stoker's *Dracula*, then to the even earlier *Carmilla* by Sheridan Le Fanu.

In those days I preferred the villainous aspects of the vampire. I recognized the erotic attraction that characters like Carmilla and Dracula had for some readers, but *I* was far more interested in the horror than the seduction. By the mid-1980s, though, when I began to write seriously myself, a change had swept over vampire literature, initiated, perhaps, by Anne Rice's 1976 novel *Interview with the Vampire*. Vamps were still dangerous, but the focus fell increasingly on their seductive and romantic qualities. The age of the antihero vampire was "dawning."

Anthology series and magazines like *Prisoners of the Night*, *Dead of Night*, and *The Vampire's Crypt* were pioneers in unleashing this new kind of vampire on the world. These were some of the magazines publishing dark fantasy and horror at the time I became interested in writing them, and by then I was ready to embrace the rising trend. Most of the stories in this collection come from that period in my writing, which is to say that the majority of vampires you'll meet here are not so much evil as they are conflicted. They do bad things; they kill and feed. But they often struggle with the "thirst," and they struggle with their own lost—or not quite lost—humanity.

I still like the really nasty vamps, and you'll meet some here, but I appreciate the complexity of character that modern vampires can display. Vampires can be many things to many people, and that has gone far toward making them the most enduring "monster" in all of literature. It's a major reason why I've visited and revisited them so many times in my work.

Finally, let me say a few more words about vampires and the erotic. Eroticism existed as part of the vampire equation from its beginnings in *Carmilla* and *Dracula* but has become far more pronounced over the last thirty years. The stories in this book follow the modern tradition, so if you don't like sex in your fiction this collection may not be for you. The descriptions range from the romantic to the graphic, although I doubt anyone who has read a Laurell K. Hamilton novel will be shocked. Still, I felt I should warn you.

So, if you're ready, welcome now to tales of Crimson and Black.

PROVERBS

BLOOD

Predation is in the bones, in the marrow. The ultimate need is for food, but even when sated a carnivore will still hunt. It wants the wet taste of life, the sweetness of watermelon flesh. Oh, it might be distracted temporarily—by games or sex. It might gather shiny baubles around it. But its need to kill isn't rational. And it won't be denied its blood.

Let the strong eat the weak. And the weak be poison.

SIN

All souls search for redemption but what if there isn't any? For the pure? Or the fallen? What if all the bodies given to glory only rot cold in the ground? And what if the greatest prayers in the most sacred books are only fossilized words, their meanings hard and empty of life? In such a world, one might be forgiven a few sins.

Let the wicked swallow the holy. And choke on them.

DEATH

In the grave there aren't any races. Everyone is a little pale. The worms love them all the same, and the carved stones above are meaningless. Corpses don't care about inscriptions. But you can bet they want the light. At least a ray of it. They want a fresh breeze to carry away their own stink. Mostly, though, they want you. Your life. Your death.

Let the dead love the living. And bury them all.

THE COLD OF
SNOW AND GHOSTS

Author's Note: The first three stories in this book, "The Cold of Snow and Ghosts," "Wanting the Mouth of a Lover," and "Vessel for the Holy," all feature the same character, a vampire named Kainja. Outside of fantasy fiction, Kainja is the only series character I've ever produced, and there is another story about him that I fully intend to write one day. It'll be the last in the series. But it's not done yet. After you read the three, there's another little note explaining something else about Kainja that I want you to know.

He ran northward across the frozen tundra, with the pure light of the Aurora streaming above him in broad arcs that sparked green and red with ionization. His flying feet seemed barely to skim the ground, leaving behind prints in the snow that were as delicate as fallen petals, and as ephemeral. Over his shoulder hung a caribou stag with its throat wrapped in a necklace of frozen black blood.

He hoped he would be in time.

In the papal courts of the Borgias, his name had been Joachim Martel. At the side of the German Chancellor Bismarck, he had simply been called Krieg. Now, in the frozen north of the Americas, with two world wars behind him, he was known to the Inuit as Kainja. They feared him as a devil—because his skin held the appearance of snow and he dwelt in the cold night where only ghosts and devils dwelt. Sometimes the native peoples even told stories about him. And sometimes he came right up to the walls of the snow houses and listened to the tales with ears that could hear the blood coursing through the hearts behind the ice blocks.

In the spring he was said to have ridden on a narwhal as it fought with an orca for its life. He had loped with wolves before the black and gray bruise of a massing storm; the hunters had heard him howling and knew his voice by its unique pitch. He had eaten snow at the birthing place of the seals, where the fine ivory powder was turned to crimson sludge from the afterbirth of ten thousand parturitions. In the fall he had been seen pirouetting on the backs of a running herd of caribou, had slept in the den of Kakwik, the wolverine who was his supposed servant, had taken sled dogs while they drowsed in a curled ball with their mates. In the winter he had eaten children. The stories were all true, except for the first and the last. He was no devil, and he did not feed on children.

He hoped he would be in time.

The being known as Kainja had crossed a wealth of miles tonight with the gall of time riding him. And there had been other miles in the nights before, all for one caribou. Though he had hoped for more. He had even traveled in the few short hours of the northern winter's day, through the weak light of an arctic sun that still held enough vigor to generate an uncomfortable heat on skin that could not sweat, on eyes that could not tear. But he had to make it north in time, in enough time to fend off the starvation overtaking the nineteen members of the Inuit band of Powhuktuk, where lived the dark-eyed Konala with her parents.

A week ago, Kainja had drifted out of the winter deadness of the poles to find hunger stalking a people he had unilaterally adopted as his own. At this time of year there were only a few hours of light each day for the Inuit to hunt, and little enough to shoot at even if there'd been more time. The dogs had already been eaten. Starvation always threatened in the north, but Powhuktuk's people had been adequately supplied only weeks before when Kainja had gone into the polar night for his annual time of seclusion. Something must have broken into their caches of meat, a white bear perhaps, or maybe wolverines, for which *he* would be blamed. For whatever reason, the people had been left to boil sinews and old caribou hides for food before Kainja came once more and put his face against the igloos to read the moans of bodies in want. It was a sound/scent he knew well, though it never came so often for him as it did for humans.

Among the need-filled bodies had been that of Konala, whose soul's birth-scream had brought him to the arctic fourteen years ago. He had been living in the Yucatan jungles when he heard it, dreaming dreams scribed on Mayan stelai ages before. The scream had driven him to his knees, forced blood in spurts from his eyes and ears. He knew the voice that cried out. It belonged to his own soul, which had died centuries ago as he turned to vampire, and which was being reborn in the body of a tiny Inuit girl. He had known that such a rebirth would happen, if he waited long enough. And since that time he'd been watching over the child as she grew with a vampire's soul inside of her, a soul that offered Kainja a second chance to achieve a kind of humanity.

All these things Kainja thought about as he ran. And more. A woman had made him a vampire. In an India of two centuries later, he had met her original human spirit reincarnated in the body of an old woman who lived at the foot of the Himalayas. Out of curiosity, Kainja had temporarily aged his form so he could come to the woman in a way that would not frighten her. He wanted to study her soul, and perhaps because his wish was for knowledge rather than blood, Kainja allowed himself for the first time since his change to be with a human when his senses were not clouded by need. What he found in the embrace of those old arms, in the dry and whispering touch of those old lips, convinced him that being human could mean beauty as well as evil.

He would never have thought it so on the night he bared his chest and asked a vampire to take him. In those days he had been sick of human wickedness, his own included, and only too happy to leave humanity behind. Life with the old woman had changed those thoughts. When she died, he buried her in a glacier that had been born in the first days of humankind. Then he waited for his own soul to return.

Konala was small and ugly and loud when Kainja first saw her, but over fourteen years he had come to love her, as a child of nature, as a fragment of his own existence, as a future that they might achieve together. He could not take the soul from the girl. Even if he had been able to force himself to the act, killing her would only release the spirit. But he believed that if she willingly shared that spirit with him, in her blood and in her flesh, then they would each become something more than human *or* vampire.

Already, Kainja had visited the girl's dreams, and in a few more years, when her body and soul were old enough and strong enough, he would come to her in reality. He did not know if she would be able to love him; he would not use his glamour to coerce her. But there were beauties he could offer, things she had never felt nor seen: like the white mist of the jungle canopy at dawn, like the silverscape of the desert beneath the moon, like the silken coiling of the sea when ripped by a nightmare tempest. She would have a choice, and perhaps she would choose him. But first she had live. That was why he ran.

With hours still to travel to the Inuit encampment, an arctic storm blew up against Kainja. The fragile light of the Aurora was swallowed by flat, ugly clouds pushed by a scouring wind off the polar sea. Snow began to fall, driven by the wind until it came at him almost horizontally. A fine gruel of ice pellets and half thawed slush began to settle in his hair and rime his body. His low skin temperature could not melt the rime fast enough to keep it from building up on his muscles, and only steady movement kept his limbs from hardening within a glaze of crystalline particles that would have turned him into a prism when the sun arose.

The caribou stag over his shoulder grew stiffer and heavier

with its own accumulation of ice, slamming its weight against his spine every time he put down a foot. And the exhaustion that had been riding his back throughout the past few nights began now to rowel him with its spurs. Kainja could run farther and faster than any human, but he was not immune to pain. It wracked him now from narrow heel to pale eyes. He kept moving.

The remaining night and half the day passed while the storm raved, but when at last the sun broke the clouds it shone down hotter than Kainja had felt it in years. That heat coiled like little snakes across his skin as the near waterless tissues of his face and hands tried to sweat and failed. His eyes dried until his vision came blurred through the film of his hardening corneas. Still he ran, carrying life for the Inuit in the form of a dead beast on his shoulder. At dusk he staggered in among the igloos of Powhuktuk's people and found them empty. He dropped the stag.

In the biggest of the snow houses, Kainja knelt beside the partially finished ribs of a kayak. Nearby lay a pile of other objects, a stone smoking pipe, a hide scraper made from musk ox horn, a handful of empty brass cartridges for a .44-40 rifle. He lifted an inner jacket, called an ateegie, in which someone had been sewing up a hole recently. A bone needle was stuck in the sleeve. He had seen Konala wearing that jacket. Now it was just one of many discarded things, things that might have been useful for the people to carry if they had not been so hunger-weak. Clearly, they had left the encampment in search of food.

The lack of a living scent in the igloo told Kainja that the Inuit had gone at least three days before. Their trail would have been covered by the storm he'd fought his way through to get here. He searched the other snow huts just in case, but then returned to stand outside the biggest igloo and seek for some guide to follow. The world was still, and above him arched the stars like the points of teeth closing down upon him.

Kainja opened his mouth to show his own teeth. He closed his eyes and spread his hands to the night. In a moment, something began to flow into his awareness, something drawn in through the pores of his skin. The first sign was a whisper of electrical current dancing through the forest of fine, pale hair at his neck. The second was a jolt of pain that snapped him upright as if with the stroke of a scourger's whip.

A magnetic field coalesced around the negative pole of Kainja's body and then began to spread out over the snow in patterns of force that realigned every molecule they touched. A faint wind stirred up snow devils and drove them away across the plain in a pattern that held the vampire at its center. When Kainja opened his eyes once more he could see a trail of footprints lying like phosphor ghosts beneath the newly fallen snow. He picked up his caribou and started running north along that trail.

Within the hour—covering more ground than the Inuit could ever have hoped to cover in that time—Kainja began finding other things to mark his way, a set of traps for catching the white fox, a copper bowl from the ore deposits on Victoria Island, extra pieces of clothing that made no difference to people who were starving. He found a pair of sealskin boots, kamiks they were called, and a broken bow that now would never be mended. Farther on were nets and hides and harpoons, and an ivory comb that had belonged to Konala.

After that he began to find people. They were dead, scattered by the side of the trail where they had been left by the others. No one had the strength to build a cairn for the fallen. Even the children were placed softly in the snow when they were gone. And the mothers and the fathers went on, knowing there was nothing else to do but try to live.

Kainja forced himself to look into the faces of all the dead so he could identify them. He did not want to miss seeing Konala. The ninth and tenth bodies that he turned over belonged to the girl's parents. They had dropped together and been frozen with their faces touching at the cheeks. Kainja searched the immediate area in case Konala had stayed behind with her kin, but went on again when he found nothing. The people had taken up the rhythm of movement now. None of them would stop until they were dead.

The vampire's own movements had become more of a stumble than a run, but he regained a bit of his strength when he saw the partially collapsed wall of a crude snow house looming in front of him. It was an old place, not built by Powhuktuk's people, but it might have been enough of a lure to attract the starving Inuit. At least they would have searched it for scraps of food.

He ripped his way through the tumbled snow blocks to find that some of the people had stopped there forever. There were six bodies in the wrecked igloo, but Konala's was not among them. Nor was Powhuktuk's. Of the nineteen members of the band, Kainja had seen sixteen of them dead. Beyond the hut he found sign of the last three who lived, three pair of footprints and a single meandering line that marked where Powhuktuk dragged his rifle behind him. Kainja closed his eyes and prayed for strength, though he had no idea who it was he prayed to. After a moment, he went on without hearing an answer.

Kainja's body had never ached this much before; his mind had never lied to him as much as it did now. He saw sunlight shining through his skin and into his face. He saw white foxes floating in the air, and humps of snow that changed to snarling bears whenever his back was turned. His teeth hurt as they dripped a golden ichor down across his lips to stain his chest, and the stag over his shoulder had begun to whisper taunts in his ear. Dimly, he recognized the signs of perlerorneq, the winter insanity that sometimes struck among the Inuit. Never had he imagined that it would come to him.

Then he found the seventeenth body and that brought him back to his senses. It was Eepuk, wife of Powhuktuk, and fifty yards farther on lay her husband. Kainja put his head to the man's chest and listened, and faintly within he could hear the sound of blood freezing in the deep caverns of the body. Death had arrived only a short time before.

Powhuktuk had been the strongest of his band, and yet, beyond the dead man's form Kainja could see the tracks of a pair of small feet and the winding trail of a rifle being dragged through the snow. Konala had taken up the gun now. She was ahead of him still.

For an hour more Kainja ran north, covering distances that he could not believe a human girl of fourteen could have covered. It gave him a small hope that perhaps she lived. But when he found her at last he nearly tripped over her fallen shape in the snow. It was at a place where pack ice had filled a narrow bay of the Arctic Ocean, and it was as if the nightmare cold blowing off that ice had at last felled the girl.

Kainja dropped to his knees beside her, still carrying the stag with which he had hoped to save her. He couldn't even touch her at first, because he wasn't sure if she was dead and he didn't want to know it if she was. Instead, he used his hands like blades to rip open the caribou and pull out the heart. The flesh was frozen hard and black, and he blew on it in hopes of thawing it, cursing his vampire body and its lack of ability to generate heat.

After a handful of moments, he managed to melt a few drop-lets of the heart's blood into a crimson slush that he dribbled into Konala's mouth. He had to touch her to do that. He had to lift her head on his knee and open her lips with his fingers. She neither helped nor resisted him. And he knew she was dead.

That knowledge didn't stop him from leaning forward to blow on her cheeks and chafe her wrists. When that didn't work he grabbed her shoulders and shook her, jolting loose her parka so the dark hair came free and began to blow in the wind. He shook her and shook her. But he knew she was dead.

In the moment when the final realization of the girl's death came to him, Kainja did what he had never intended to do. He reached with long fingers and pulled back the fur at the girl's throat, then leaned forward and bit deeply through the cold skin into the left carotid. The body was not yet frozen; the veins still held a faint pulse of warmth. It was not enough. Already the foulness of death had begun to corrupt her blood. She would never rise from this place.

Kainja lifted his head and howled, and a jolt of broken images razored his thoughts. He didn't know if they were just his own conception of the girl's death, or if maybe a last piece of her soul had passed through his teeth on its way into the wine chill of the sky. He saw her last days, though. He trudged with her as she watched her people fall, people who had birthed and nurtured her, who had spoken with her every day of her life. He swallowed with her as she chewed the leggings from her boots and bit her fingers to draw blood. But she had gone on.

She had gnawed strands of her hair, torn furrows in her chest with her nails, eaten clots of ice that only made her stomach hurt all the more. But even when no other feet imprinted the snow beside hers, she had not stopped. Kainja watched in memory as fourteen-year-old Konala walked straight into the mouth of the winter, dragging behind her a gun and the tiny bit of hope it gave. Kainja wanted to weep, and it hurt him that vampires had no tears.

Kainja did not think about what Konala's death meant for his dream of regaining a piece of his soul. He just picked the girl up and began to walk north in the direction she had been heading. A little farther and he would come to a place with no sun and no days for the next few months, only nights. And in the long dark he would stand holding Konala and let the ice coat him and paint his skin even whiter than it was. He would stand until he became as stone, unable to feel the girl in his arms, or the absence of a heartbeat in the hollow of her neck. He would stand until he became one with the snow and the ghosts, until the sun would come in time and use him as a mirror to reflect its pulsing light.

Kainja had walked half a mile before he realized that he was crying after all, real tears that froze on his cheeks and fell on the body in his arms. He looked down at Konala with astonishment. The girl's soul must indeed have passed into him when he had bitten her, and some fragment of that soul seemed to have found a new home. Or an old one. It had to have been a deliberate gift, a last act of the girl's fading spirit, which knew the vampire from her dreams. Once, Kainja had prayed for such a gift. Now he wept for it.

WANTING THE
MOUTH OF A LOVER

I.

There were seven bells ringing, three of iron, three of brass—one of silver. Their sound was as chaotic and cold as the wind that blew at Kainja's back, as sharp and dark as the scimitar shapes of the mountain vultures circling above his head in the dimming sky of evening. Those vultures had a purpose here, but it wasn't that they were waiting for him to die. That would have been futile. They were waiting for him to leave so they could settle again to the feast he had interrupted.

That feast laid spread on bare rocks in front of Kainja. It was the crumpled and torn bodies of ten Buddhist monks, their orange robes stained into rust by their own blood. They had been arranged to form a mandala, but if that shape was meant to represent the cosmos, it was a perverted cosmos. On the chest of each of the dead lay a tiny cairn built from his heart and genitals. And at the center of the mandala, at the point of reintegration, sat the bleached skull of a snow leopard on which a left-handed swastika—a sauvastika—had been scrawled in red.

Kainja had known the swastika as a good fortune symbol long before the German Hitler had corrupted it. He had seen it here in the Himalayas, and on the coins of old Mesopotamia. He had found it among Mayan ruins, and in sand paintings of the Navajo and Hopi. But he knew that even the ancients drew a distinction between left-handed and right-handed, between a luck symbol that rotated clockwise, and one that turned the other way into night and vile magic. The druids had called that direction widdershins, and they had certainly understood some things about darkness.

Framing the meticulously ordered canvas of the dead were a monastery's ruins. Smoke helices lifted over broken walls and orange and black kites fluttered on the ground like raped angels. A row of stone monkeys had lost their heads. Even worse was the water cistern filled with blood, a conspicuous waste. Someone had created a sadistic landscape here. They had done it deliberately, out of some need or passion that Kainja did not understand and which horrified him. And the worst thing of all was that only one person could be responsible, the woman Kainja loved more than anyone else living in the world.

II.

Kainja recalled a pale cathedral of ice. Meltwater had sculpted it from a glacier and the woman Ryjul had made it a gallery for her art. In the walls were frozen ten thousand bones she had gathered, bones of fresh white and sun-faded ivory, bones black with fossilization. The woman had not killed for them. She had only found them and put them in the ice to make skeleton creatures both fragile and lovely, creatures that had never lived but should have. There had been a mouse with a hawk's wings, and Kainja had known when he saw it that he would love the being who created it.

III.

Kainja turned his mind away from memories and toward the violence at his feet. Ryjul had created this canvas too. He recognized the style as surely as if she had signed it, though here her art was overlain by a brutality it had never before possessed. She had not found these dead. She had made them.

Kainja looked up from the ruins, past the vultures with their bladed wings, past the darkening valley to where a chill wind swept like a broom across the snowfields of the Great Himalayan Range. There lay the swelling curve of the Khumbu Glacier, bright in the sun, with the peak of Cho Oyu to the west and white Everest to the east. He would have to go up that glacier, but the trail would be easily followed. It would be marked by the smell of shed blood.

That was when Kainja noticed the sky and realized it was free of vultures. He turned to see if the scavengers had landed, but found that their larder had emptied itself instead. Behind him, silently, the ten monks had risen to their feet and were watching him, swaying gently from side to side as if rocked by an invisible hand. Their mouths were open and their teeth were long. Their feet didn't touch the ground.

IV.

Kainja recalled Ryjul telling him that he was beautiful. It was no pleasing symmetry of face she was referring to. It was only that he was like her art in a way she loved. Kainja was a duality, a vampire who often seemed more human than the true humans she had known. He was two things, like Ryjul's art, like Ryjul herself. Though she was no vampire.

On that day of her remark, Ryjul had stripped off her robes of straw and grass and had come to him to make love. But it was as if she wanted to love another artist's creation, and Kainja had been unwilling to fill that role. Instead, he waited for her sculptor's sense of his form to disappear behind her pure joy in being with him as flesh. Then he came to her, and took away her robes with hands he'd warmed in the fire.

He remembered how she had touched him that day, that night, on the morning that followed. It was as if she had crawled inside his skin and animated his cold-dead body with the zephyr warmth of her own spirit. He was like her art, and—like in her art—she couldn't accept anything that was dead without trying to give it back some echo of life.

V.

And now? Kainja glanced at the orange robed monks as they began to drift slowly toward him like kites on a thermal breeze. He wondered if Ryjul was animating the dead again, with motives more sinister and dread.

As if answering his thoughts, Kainja heard a distant laugh tinkle down from the sky. It aroused three emotions in him, anger, fear, relief. The anger and fear came because he knew whose laugh he was hearing, and the relief came because it wasn't Ryjul. Relief was the shortest lived of the three, however. It lasted only until he remembered that Ryjul's hands had been the ones to arrange a mandala from the dead. Then the monks flashed toward him like a flock of predatory birds and he turned his mind to defense.

A surge of power tightened Kainja's spine. He hoped it would be enough to save him, but doubts roweled his mind. There were things he had both won and lost this past year. He had won a piece of his reincarnated human soul when a girl he had loved in dreams surrendered to arctic cold but granted him a fragment of her spirit. He had lost...other things, things incompatible with humans and souls. He hoped his glamour wasn't one of them, and he lifted his hands and spread his fingers to find out.

A blast of wind whipped from beneath Kainja's boots, hurling dust and small pebbles before it as it raced to meet the oncoming monks. Those attackers slowed, slowed, as if the air they were swimming in had suddenly begun to congeal. More dust lifted. And bigger rocks were moving too, shards of flint and granite, chunks of limestone incised with fossils.

The monks were forced back, their blood-stained robes snapping in the gale. But in the next instant those robes ripped away and the attackers surged forward again, spreading out around their target to come at him from all sides. Kainja snarled, feeling a seldom tasted rage wet his lips. He released the vampire.

Kainja was not metamorphic, as some vampires were. The paleness of his skin and the fangs that were usually folded back into his mouth were permanent fixtures of his body. His alterations were internal, driven by the flux of electromagnetic currents and by chemical changes in his brain. The only outward sign was a flickering discharge of light that coalesced around his form, as if the air flowing past him was being heated to the point of luminescence.

The attacking creatures didn't recognize Kainja's alterations until too late. The corona surrounding the vampire stabilized, brightened. Kainja began to spin on his heels, hands out, fingers hooked into the air. Streaks of iridescence erupted where his hands were moving, as if his nails had torn holes in curtains hiding a rainbow. Sapphire. Emerald. Aquamarine. The air started to crystallize, with Kainja as the seed.

The crystal's growth was explosive, like snowflake shrapnel whipped outward by some monstrous detonation. Kainja's enemies were nothing more than impurities in the solution; even the carbon in their lungs began to jewel. The effect was devastating as soft tissues ruptured.

Then, streamers of amber lightning crackled along the faceted planes of the swelling crystal, ripping into and through the disintegrating bodies of the monks. The lightning turned red, like ore veins of ruby, and twisted around on itself to feed back upon Kainja where he stood in the center of the crystalline lattice. He screamed when the bolts struck him, but it was a savage scream, a scream full of lust.

Kainja's pores opened as the bloody light flowed into him, painting his cells, surging into his brain. His pupils dilated, turning as black as obsidian scalpels, leaving the whites like bruised pearls. It had been long and long since Kainja had fed in this way, and the pleasure was almost more than he could handle. His mouth opened; his teeth extended fully. He began to laugh and the sound was not human.

For a moment, Kainja forgot what he had been trying to achieve for the past many centuries. He forgot compassion, and love. His eyes looked on the destruction he had wrought, and they found it good. His laughter became a roar, a gale, a storm of winged echoes beating on the mountains. But some memory tugged at him and spiked thorns into the bubble of his rage. The crystal shattered and he fell to his knees.

VI.

Kainja recalled human warmth in all its forms. He remembered soft lips fevered by illness, and griddle hot tears on a child's cheeks. He remembered the heat in the bodies of lovers, remembered how it changed from one moment to the next, from one curve of skin to another. He remembered Ryjul. She had worn her warmth like a cloak, despite the coldness to which her deformity had exposed her in growing up.

VII.

And now it was memories of Ryjul that struggled within Kainja to keep him from turning rogue. He didn't want to be vampire or human. He wanted to be both. On his knees, Kainja closed his eyes and hammered against the melee of emotions sweeping through him—hate, lust, hunger. Hunger was strongest. He needed to feed. He *wanted* to feed. He thought of Ryjul's throat, of the heart that fluttered just beneath her breasts.

"She asked you once to take her," a voice teased in his mind. "She always wanted you to. Besides...you saw the mandala. She deserves it now, after what she's done."

It was the final two sentences that opened Kainja's eyes, and his pupils were contracted and the whites clear. He knew those last thoughts were not his. And he knew who they belonged to. He leaned forward and vomited light and blood onto the ground.

An icy silver chuckle drew Kainja's attention. On a block of fallen masonry sat a vampire, tall, blond, with eyes like scars in an otherwise handsome face. As Kainja watched, the vampire stood and paced over to one of the broken monks. He reached down and plucked the fangs, then tossed them lightly in his hand as if weighing whether or not they would fit the necklace of other teeth hanging around his neck.

"Danzeg," Kainja said. "I *thought* you might be behind this."

"Not at all. Just helping a friend."

"You're lying. Ryjul would never be a friend to you. Not without trickery."

"Oh? She came to me. True, she seemed somehow under the impression that you and I were close. But, impressions or not, she wanted what I offered." Danzeg shrugged. "Surely though, you knew she loved you. She wanted to be just like you."

"Only...the poison in your blood made her into something else."

Danzeg smiled with cold teeth. "I'll admit to drinking a bit deeply for my part. It made her hungry. Why, she almost drained me when I gave her my throat."

Kainja winced. He knew how intoxicating it was to take even a little blood from another vampire. And he'd had centuries to develop tolerance. How must it have been for Ryjul, callow as she was? Danzeg had fed her enough to drive her insane.

"She'll fight your poison," Kainja said. "And win!"

"You're a fool to believe that. She tried to resist when the hunger first came over her. But in the end I had to cuff her from my throat. And now," he gestured at the ruined monastery, "I think she's beginning to see the beauty in following my ways."

"There's never been any beauty in your ways, Danzeg. Everything you are and have done is ugly."

"You created me," Danzeg shouted, his composure punctured by sudden anger. "You created me in an attempt to assuage your ancient and petty guilt, to prove that your crime, like mine, was not so terrible that it put you beyond redemption. If there is a flaw in me. If there is ugliness in me. It must have been in you first."

"I would not dispute you," Kainja said. "It is only that I try to hide my ugliness instead of flaunting it as you do."

"Such noble words from one who has made a principle of interfering with human affairs. And of failing. Eh, Joachim Martel? How did your sweet intrigues save Italy from the

Borgias? Or should I call you Krieg and ask how well you stopped the spread of militarism in Germany of a century ago? Or perhaps I should use a still older name, one to remind you of who is truly full of ugliness."

"Whatever you call me doesn't change who I am now," Kainja said. "Even though I failed often in past days, it doesn't change what I intended. And yes, I created you. I owed you something for that, and I paid for years in hopes you would grow beyond your urges. I won't pay anymore. And if I could take back what I gave you I would."

"But you can't, can you? I'm too powerful now. I know what you know, and I learned more on my own. You can't touch me. But," Danzeg glanced up toward Ryjul's glacier home, "I can still touch you."

Kainja fought down both despair and rage. He held out his hand to the other vampire, for one last time. "Danzeg." The name rolled off Kainja's tongue like a prayer. "Did you know there is an ancient language in which that word means beloved son? I gave it to you as a name, though there was a time when I wanted the title for myself.

"I once did an evil thing. And I was ready to atone for it with my death when a woman came and offered me an alternative. I was so sick of human corruption, my own included, that I took her offer. Only then did I learn the nature of true corruption. It took time, but I grew past that. And ever since I've tried to live differently, though often failing.

"Then I saw you about to be executed for a crime that seemed at first no different from mine. You were right about why I made you a vampire. I thought we were the same. And if I could create goodness in you then I would prove worthy of redemption. But our crimes were different. Mine was worse in many ways, but I had never given up my humanity as you and the other Nazis did. Changing you was a mistake. But it can be rectified if you come to me now."

"Fool," Danzeg said. "In barely fifty years I've come near to surpassing you. Think of what I'll be in another fifty, or in the fifty after that. In the meantime...." He glanced once more to the heights. "Why not go see your lover. I'm sure she's anxious to love you again."

Danzeg turned away as Kainja felt wetness bleed into his eyes. The younger vampire threw back his head and the last of the sunlight struck him and began to sleet right through his skin. In that moment Danzeg cast no shadow; in another he was gone. A predatory wind stirred the ashes of the monastery and caused its bells to ring. Kainja trembled.

VIII.

A tea-black night enfolded Kainja as he followed a long path up the glacier, and after a while his legs became machinery and his mind drifted into memories. He recalled swords and saddles and blood, and deadly nightshade dripped into wine. He remembered the purr-rumble of distant artillery, and tanks churning through fields of wheat. He remembered a young girl named Konala, who had died despite his attempts to protect her.

Danzeg was right. All his meddling in human affairs had resulted in failure. He had never saved anyone. So how could he hope to save Ryjul now from the venom coursing within her. And yet, giving up would be a betrayal of his beliefs. He could not live with that. Not again.

IX.

Where a granite cliff peeked from an icy bed, Kainja found a cave's mouth. Ryjul would be inside. And just outside in the glacier would be the frozen grotto where she kept her art. Kainja wondered what kind of art hung there now, and he was afraid to look. Instead, he slid down to the black throat of the cavern and entered.

A darkness deeper than night filled the space inside the mountain, but Kainja's eyes could pierce it. They found Ryjul, a different Ryjul than he had known before. The Ryjul of old had been cruelly stooped, with a twisted body from a hard birth. This new Ryjul stood tall and straight-spined, with onyx hair trailing down her back to her waist. She stood facing away from him, deft fingers working on something in her hands, and Kainja saw what it was when she heard him and turned around. She was holding the torn head of a man and sewing snow leopard fangs into his pupils.

Ryjul's glance sparked a vampire's red and she dropped her work and held out her hands in welcome. "My love. Come. See how I've changed." Her voice was chocolate sweet, enticing, filled with a hunger that had alloyed itself with sexual arousal. It had no effect on Kainja. He had heard such voices many times and knew them as cliché. He much preferred the honest rasp that had once fought its way from this woman's throat.

"Ryjul! What have you done?"

The woman threw back her shoulders, thrusting out full breasts on a chest that had been withered. "Don't you like it?" she purred.

And again it was something Kainja had seen and heard before. How he hated the posturings of lust, as if they could fill a need for more than the few moments it took to consummate the act.

"No," he told her.

"I doubt that," she said, as she swayed toward him.

Kainja let her approach and put her arms around his neck, but when she would have pulled him down into a kiss he resisted. She was strong, immensely so, but it wasn't enough to match the strength he'd been building for centuries. He grasped her hands and pried them apart. She stepped back, and for a moment her eyes turned a human brown and whispered with fear. Then the vampire took her again and she snarled into his face.

"What is wrong with you? This is how you wanted me! You cared nothing for the cripple I was before."

"Not true," he said, reaching out a palm. "I loved her."

"Liar!" she shrieked, batting his arm aside. "If you had loved her you wouldn't have left her."

"I left her because she asked me to change her forever. And I wanted her as she was."

Ryjul's anger guttered away. Her hands fell to her sides and her mouth worked until words spilled free. "I only hoped to be like you," she said. "To have what you had. Was that so much to ask?"

Kainja grabbed her hand and lifted it in front of her face. Her nails were dark with the dried blood of those she'd slaughtered. "Is this what you wanted," he demanded.

In a moment of insight, Ryjul shuddered. "But had it been you instead of Danzeg," she said. "Maybe then—"

"Maybe not. I created Danzeg, remember?"

Ryjul shuddered again and shook her head to clear her thoughts. She was still resisting her vampire needs, meaning that her human soul had not yet been driven from her body. That stalemate could not last. Danzeg's poison would soon be boiling inside of her, triggering a surge of hunger. She'd want Kainja's blood then, and if she got it her soul would be burned away and her mind would be locked forever in crimson thirst.

Had the sharing of vampire and human blood been carried out over months, had it been accompanied by the sharing of mouths and bodies and love, then Ryjul's mind would have survived. But the sudden change induced by Danzeg would tear her apart, and leave her insane if she lived. There was only one way for Kainja to stop it, but he had to have Ryjul's acceptance in order to try.

He walked over and picked up the head she had been working on. It began to glow as he touched it, filling with harsh crimson light.

"Is this your art now?" he demanded. "Or maybe it lies in that heated moment when your hands go inside a living body and kill it. Tell me!"

Ryjul didn't answer, and in anger Kainja ripped the fangs from the eyes and hurled the head aside. He closed his fist over the teeth and squeezed until his hand was bloodless, and when he opened his palm again the teeth had been replaced by a tiny figurine of ivory, by a mouse with the wings of a hawk.

Kainja turned his hand over and dropped the miniature. And while it fell, twinkling with its own light, he watched a war go on in Ryjul's face. He watched a snarl turn to a frown, turn to a smile, turn to a gasp of dismay. And with a movement too swift to follow, the woman lunged forward and caught the tiny image before it shattered on the stone.

Ryjul looked up at Kainja then. Her eyes swirled with color—black, brown, firefly red. But for this moment they were mostly brown. "I didn't know it would be like this," she whispered. And the voice was her old voice, raspy and raw. Just as he had loved it.

"I was afraid it would," Kainja replied.

"I don't know how long I can resist the need. I might do worse than the monastery next time."

"I won't let that happen," Kainja said, as he moved toward her and knelt to brush the hair from her neck. His teeth were already exposed and they punctured her skin like a needle. Ryjul shivered, her voice whispering a mantra of uncoupled words. Kainja ventured deeper into her veins, searching out Danzeg's poison and drawing it into himself. His body moved over hers, into hers, shaping itself to unknown contours. Pores opened with a flow of electrical current that spidered like a web of light between their skins.

Ryjul began to sob quietly, though she was vampire enough so that no tears streaked her face. Among vampires only Kainja could cry, because he carried within himself a piece of pure soul. And now he bled the tears that Ryjul wanted to bleed. Until, as the toxins slowly left Ryjul's body and entered Kainja's, the man's tears dried and the woman's eyes grew wet. At last, Kainja lifted himself away from Ryjul and looked upon her damp face, as damp as only a cleansed soul could make it. He smiled, and kissed the woman until she slept.

X.

Kainja stood at the mouth of Ryjul's cave, recalling nothing. He understood what he had given up this night. A year ago he had regained a fragment of his own soul. Tonight he'd drowned that fragment in Danzeg's poison.

Or should I call him by his true name? he thought. *Should I call him Quisling? Once a traitor, always a traitor.*

But then Kainja held up the ivory figurine he'd removed from Ryjul's sleeping hand. He smiled a vampire's smile and tossed it into the cold air where its tiny wings began to beat with a sound like distant bells. He watched it fly away.

Once a traitor, always a traitor.

Or perhaps not!

On this night, Judas Iscariot had refused to betray another friend.

VESSEL FOR THE HOLY

I.

In a still place on a mountain's side, amid a caravan of boulders left from a time of ancient ice, the vampire stood alone. His name was Kainja. Night's face was dark and fair around him, comfortable like an old friend. A mistral breeze rilled down from above, licking his cheeks with the taste of snow and wintry spice. He was here in response to a summons written in a language dead to all but his own kind. Yet, no one had come to meet him. Though he had waited long.

To the east a few miles lay an abbey whose name he did not know. Men and women—humans—would be at late prayers there. Here it lay all empty and silent. Except for the wind.

He turned to leave, and stopped again as footsteps punctured holes in the quiet. The steps distracted him and he felt too late the sweep of the attack that came from behind. One blow hammered his skull, lifting him bodily and throwing him a dozen yards down the mountain to drop like a broken bird. From there he went down into a darkness that was not so friendly.

II.

Kainja fought the recall of his memories, fought his tongue when it would have voiced those memories to the air. But the sweet, sweet words that dripped into his ears were insistent, insidious, irresistible.

"Remember for me. Love. Remember...remember... remember."

He did as the words commanded, wishing all the while that he was deaf and could not hear the sound of his voice as it babbled and babbled, as it revealed truths better kept hidden.

"Dust. There was dust. The sky black at noon. Rope hanging in the sick, dead light. Near the Place of Skulls. I died, did not die. Oh God, don't make me remember."

"But you will, Kainja. You must. For all our sakes."

He tried to open his eyes to see the speaker. Could not do so. The controls of his body were locked away in a place he couldn't reach, though he sensed no restraints, no drugs. Only his voice worked, and that under the direction of the woman who stood so near that the scent from her veins spilled into his nostrils.

"The blood," he said. "Years of blood. Pale wounds. Licked clean. Filled. Hollow. Filled. Vessels for the holy. Chalices to be emptied. Profaned on my tongue. The pulse in throats, breasts, thighs. Eyes wet. Afraid with love. Bodies straining in their silks. The mouths of women. Of men. Children."

The speaker again: "Give me the names, Kainja." Her words chimed soft as a bell muffled in lace. "All the names in your blood."

There was no resisting. Kainja heard his voice telling, telling. He could not gauge the passing of time, though he knew it was long. Sometimes the words quit, whenever the speaker quit and went away. But always they started again, after an hour or a day. His body began taking back its strength, began responding sluggishly to his demands. Once more he felt the touch and flow of voltages over his skin. He began to struggle, until straps buckled him to a table that he discovered only from its shape.

Still his voice droned. It seemed years before he ran down. By that time he was more empty than he had ever been, with all his memories bled out into the world. Even so, his throat still constricted, tried to open. He gasped with nothing else to say, like a fish left behind when its stream moved on.

A hand touched his mouth, his throat, soothed them into stillness. "Sleep," the speaker said. "The struggle is over. You've done well."

Kainja knew what he'd done. And it had not been "well." He wanted to die but he had wanted that many times before and it had never happened. His body relaxed, as the speaker had ordered. His mind followed. He slept.

III.

It was morning when Kainja awoke. Even without windows he could tell, by the heat pulsing in the air, by the lyric whisper that the sun poured into the sky. He had never found another who heard that sound, though to him it was a clear and powerful music thrumming in his bones. At times he enjoyed it. Today was not one of those times. His mind and body ached as if they had been hewn apart and left to grow back together on their own.

A laboratory surrounded him; wallet-thick straps held him bound to a padded table that was cool as his skin. Computers filled a nearby desk. The rococo shapes of more equipment gathered around in a half circle. He recognized a polygraph and oscilloscope, for measuring brain waves and heart rates. He wasn't sure why the other pieces were there, pieces with names like spectrograph and gene sequencer.

Kainja tried his bonds but could not break them. Even at full strength he might not have been able to do so, and he was certainly not at full strength now. He was hungry.

Unlike many others of his kind, Kainja resisted the blood hunger—almost always. He knew all vampires could do the same, if they willed it. If necessary, their bodies would draw nourishment from the electromagnetic energy that flowed unseen all around them. They might suffer, as he would suffer, but after the agony of dying there could be no other pain to match. So now he put the red thoughts away where he could feel them crawling but not respond.

The door opened and a woman came through. She was ill from some disease that peeked out through her gaunt skin, that showed itself in her limp brown hair. Over a gray skirt and a gray nylon blouse she wore a lab coat. Kainja was immediately aware that she was the speaker to whom he'd told everything.

On the woman's hand was a wedding ring. He thought nothing of it until he realized that she was unlikely to be married. Her scent betrayed her virginity, even though her years had clearly passed forty. Then he realized what she was, and inwardly he shrank. She would have learned enough about him to discover his birth name—Judas Iscariot. He wondered how a nun would react to such knowledge, given that she had wed herself to Jesus Christ.

The woman flipped on a light and started across the lab toward him. She stopped in surprise when she found him awake.

"Oh!" Her thin face filled out with a smile and the bones of her disease retreated for the moment back beneath firm flesh. Pleasure poured into her brandy-colored eyes. It was not the response Kainja had expected.

She walked over to stand near him. "I've waited for this," she said. "But I thought it would come at night."

Kainja wasn't in any mood to be generous, even to a nun. "Vampires are under no compulsion to be nocturnal. But I imagine you know that after raping my memories."

He hoped his words would punish her, remind her that she held him bound and had gone through his secrets like a voyeur. The attempt succeeded. Her illness crawled back into her face, draining it of any smile. Kainja felt a surge of irrational guilt. She was lovely, he realized, and wondered at the sudden intensity of his warmth toward her. She had plundered him but he could not hate her. A thread of...something was drawn tight between them. How had he come to be here, in her power? He couldn't remember.

"Actually no," she was saying. "Never thought to ask that question. I guess I assumed that.... Well, that vampires were just that way."

Kainja didn't know whether to believe her or not. He couldn't recall everything he had told her. Perhaps she *hadn't* asked that question, which would mean she wasn't a trained interrogator. But then why had she been pressing him about his past so intently? And what purpose was served by the scientific instruments filling this lab?

He had imagined himself imprisoned by one of his own kind. Or by the tool of one such. This woman did not know enough to be a tool. If she still believed vampires were compelled to sleep in the day, what other myths might she buy? Would she threaten him with a crucifix next? He hoped not. It wouldn't trouble him physically, but there were some betrayals one never got over feeling guilty about. He decided it wouldn't hurt to let her believe a few legends.

"I'm older than most," he said. "More tolerant of things."

"Very old! Yes, I know. But tell me about the tolerances you've developed." She seemed to want to shift the conversation from the personal to the objective. Her hand plucked a pen from her coat pocket as if she were going to take notes.

"No," Kainja said. She wasn't going to escape that easily.

The woman looked...hurt. "Why are you so angry?" she asked. "I haven't harmed you."

Kainja sputtered, a very human response that might have embarrassed him had he taken note of it. "Haven't harmed me! You tie me down, pick apart my memories while I can't resist. What euphemism do you use? Release me. Let me decide myself whether to answer your questions or not."

"You don't—" she started to say. But some thought touched her voice and shut off her words. The hurt was part of it too, though Kainja didn't understand it.

"I can't release you yet," she stated at last.

"My turn to ask why?"

"I didn't intend— Well, there's something I can't let you... interfere with."

"And what might that be?"

She smiled, but the gesture was fleeting and held no humor. She had withdrawn her emotion from him and it didn't make sense he should be so bothered by that.

"Information for information," she said. "Answer my questions and I'll answer yours."

He stared at her, wondering if she were seeking for weaknesses. "Tell me your name first," he blurted.

After a pause, she nodded. "I'm Sister Judith."

Kainja felt his skin tighten. The name! So like his own from before. And like Judas Iscariot, this woman had her own fearful secret. She was swollen with it. And it scared him. He'd felt the same around fanatics before. People like this could destroy the world. Or save it.

"All right," he said, needing to know more. "Some questions, I'll answer."

"What have you become more tolerant of?" She spoke as if gathering information was a habit, as if she no longer cared about answers.

"Sunlight," he said. Because she expected it. "I can't sweat." (The truth.) "So the sun heats me faster than a human." (Also true.) "But I've adjusted over the years." (A lie. He'd always been this way.)

"What else?"

He didn't tell her about his resistance to the blood hunger. Or that his body cells could feed on electrical current. That information might be useful. Instead, he said: "Humans. I tolerate them much better than I used to. I've even grown to like a few."

She didn't respond to the probe of humor in his words, though he found himself wanting her to. "What about—" she started.

"Sorry," he interrupted. "We're trading here. Remember? What is it that I could interfere with?"

Her eyes surveyed him. She was wondering what to give him, how much fiction to mix with her truth. It was to be expected.

"I'll tell you some of it," she said after a moment. "I found an odd thing about your blood. You probably know the four human blood groups—A, B, AB, O. They're pretty stable. I'm

'A,' for example. I could take a transfusion of type 'O' without any problem. And it wouldn't alter how I made new blood. It would all still be type 'A.' You're not the same. Your blood is like a composite of all the people you've...uh...."

"Bitten?"

"I didn't want to say it, but yes. The people you've bitten. It's like a type 'A' getting a transfusion of 'O' and becoming type 'AO.' Each time you take blood your own plasma changes. It's...a sort of memory."

"A memory?"

"That's how I'd put it. Luckily, you remember red and white blood cells both."

Excitement had drawn Judith this far into her explanation, but now Kainja saw her hesitate. She was about to close herself up against him and he exerted his glamour to stoke her passion for her work, to keep her talking. Pores opened; spider webs of current wove through his skin. She would see it as light, as beauty.

"Why luckily?" he asked, smiling gently.

She smiled too, and her hesitation passed. She rushed on. "Because white blood cells are the key to everything. They're much more complex than red blood cells. They contain DNA. They—" She stopped talking abruptly, her eyes going flat with the recognition that she'd said too much. "You manipulated me," she accused. Again there was hurt in her voice, and Kainja felt sick knowing what he had done and seeing how vulnerable she was.

Then sparks of realization arced through every nerve in his body. *Blood cells*! *DNA*! His gaze swiveled from Judith's face to a machine near his head. "Gene Sequencer," he read. His muscles surged, pitted themselves against the straps holding him down. The straps won. He slumped.

Judith had stepped back, sudden fear of him turning her face strange, bringing her illness rushing to the surface.

"You can't do this," Kainja stated.

She misunderstood him. Accidentally or intentionally, he

couldn't tell.

"Why?" she snapped, her fear mutating into anger. "Because I'm a nun? I have a doctorate in genetics. This lab," she waved her hand around, "is next door to one of the biggest research universities in the country. Anything I need, I can get. I've done things here no one else has ever done."

"The consequences—"

"You don't have a clue what the consequences will be!" She was shouting now. "Well I do. You've carried history in your blood for two thousand years. *History*! Not myth. I've already sequenced the oldest DNA in your body other than your own. From that I made an embryo, a perfect clone of the first person whose blood you drank."

Kainja, too, was angry. He shook his head. "And what do you think you're going to get?" he asked brutally. "You think you're going to grow *Jesus* in your test tube? I never touched his blood. He's not there to find. But it doesn't matter. All you've got is some old DNA. Your clone won't have memories of the past. Those aren't in the genes."

This time Judith's thin smile lasted longer, though it still held no warmth. She didn't seem disturbed by his words. And he thought that, of course, she already knew everything he'd said. He'd missed something.

"You've never really believed in anything, have you?" she asked. "I'm sorry for that. Like I said, I've already sequenced the DNA, created the embryo. I carried it myself. The baby was born perfectly healthy. That was eight years ago, two years after I brought you here."

She turned and walked away.

Kainja felt destroyed. To know that a child had been cloned from his blood. That Judith had carried it. To hear that he'd lost ten years of time. All those truths hammered him.

"Wait!" he shouted after the woman. But she didn't speak or respond. He'd driven her away. She passed out the door, turning off the light and leaving Kainja alone with his thoughts and the dark.

IV.

Kainja did not sleep again, and Judith did not return. His hunger, dormant during the long quiet years, grew now until it was a savage tide that threatened to overwhelm his intellect. He fought, and abruptly the tide receded as his cells adjusted to a starvation diet drawn from the electromagnetic energy in the air. He was left fragile but whole.

All through the next weeks Kainja worked against his bonds, pulling, wearing, stretching, abrading—toiling like a machine. Two months passed before the straps parted and he rose from his bed of ten years. The house had been boarded up but he tore through a window to set himself free. He began to search.

Before another year had passed he found Sister Judith and the clone she had made from his blood. Any anger he might have felt toward the woman was gone. No matter what she'd done to him as her captive, she'd tried to protect him in the end. In searching for her trail he'd discovered a trust fund set up to keep the house and its lab from being rented or sold for twenty years. She had known he would escape eventually.

When he did discover her—using both the tools of technology and of a knowledge far more ancient—it was in the Holy Land, in Jerusalem. Perhaps he should have guessed.

V.

Kainja arrived in Jerusalem feeling the weight of his two thousand years. He had never returned here in all that time. Now it hurt him to put his feet on these streets, to see the golden-yellow facings of the buildings, so much the color that he remembered. Most would have named the color a warm one. To him it was cold.

He passed the Damascus Gate and the walls of the Old City, moving always toward the point where his senses told him Sister Judith would be. Only once did he deviate from a straight line, when he came to the Via Dolorosa, the Road of Sorrows that

Jesus had taken on his way to the cross. There, he turned aside to seek another route.

In a small house little different from other poor ones in the city, Kainja found Judith again. She lay gaunt in bed, death resting quietly within her in the sure knowledge that she was almost his. In all ways that Kainja counted, she was more beautiful than ever.

When he slipped through her open window she smiled and held out to him a stiff and trembling hand. He took it, recognizing the genuineness of her emotion. She was pleased to see him; as he was her. Kainja was no longer surprised at his feelings for this woman, though he couldn't explain them.

Judith's voice rasped when she spoke, as if it could hardly be contained in her frail body. But her words and meaning were clear.

"I'm glad you escaped. I knew you would. Though not how long it might take. A dozen times I almost came back. But I waited too late." She raised a stick-like arm. "I gave myself this. Somehow during the cloning procedure. But I don't care. I always felt that you'd make it in time."

"In time for what?"

"My death. Joshua will need someone to look after him then."

Kainja winced when he heard that name. He wondered if Judith understood its significance, felt sure that she did.

"So you bore a son?"

"Yes, of course. A fine one."

"And you'd trust me to care for him? Have you forgotten what I am? *Who* I am?"

"I remember who you *were*. And for that reason alone I think you'll take better care of Joshua than anyone else in the world. Especially now that certain…forces have become aware of his existence. Besides, what kind of woman would I be if I didn't trust the man I'd loved for over ten years."

Kainja's eyes burned with dryness. He wished for tears. But in that the two of them were alike now. Years ago he had cried, but the glands were long dormant. And Judith's disease had eaten her ability to cry.

Kainja lowered his gaze, breaking the visual lock between them. "I feel some of what you feel," he said. "But how can you say that what you did to me was love?"

Judith shook her head, the effort sketching pain into her face. "You didn't understand when you woke. Your memory was damaged. I *found* you that way. One night when I was praying in the mountains. I thought for an instant that you were an angel. Literally! Your skin. Your beauty."

She smiled, as if reliving the scene. "The sinful thoughts I had! Just from looking at you. Sinful because of who and what I was, not because of you. I don't know what I might have done if you'd been well. But you were hurt. Your brain was hurt. In some terrible battle I felt lucky to have missed.

"It took almost ten years for your mind to heal. I was amazed it could, but I guess there are advantages to being a vampire. Every night I talked to you. It was the only way I could reach you. And I made you talk to me because it helped you find a way back.

"Oh, I studied you too, of course. Couldn't help that. When I learned about your blood I knew the touch of God was in our meeting. I believed! That's why I did, what I did."

"But I thought—" Kainja started. "But you bound me," he finished.

"As you healed you struggled so hard I was afraid you'd hurt yourself. That day when you awoke I would have freed you. But your anger frightened me. Not for myself. I don't think. But for Joshua. It never occurred to me that you would think me your captor. I should have known."

"How could you," Kainja said. "And I gave you no chance to explain."

"I was angry with you too. Silly. I…. Well, I told you I was in love with you. Oh, I'm sure it was partly because you were a safe target in your coma. But there was more to it. I always realized. That day I felt rejected."

"I'm sorry."

"No need. You weren't responsible for my expectations."

"No. Now *you* don't understand. I'm sorry because I knew when I first saw you that there was a bond between us. I drove you away in spite of it. Not the first time I've been a fool."

Sister Judith squeezed his hand. "The important thing is not where we started, but that you ended up here. And I want you to meet Joshua. He is a part of you, after all."

"I'm here, Mother." A small but sturdy voice spoke from the doorway behind them. "I heard you talking."

Kainja stiffened, then turned slowly to see a boy of about nine years standing quietly and still at the threshold of the room. Even in the dim light Kainja could easily make out the eyes within the sun-darkened but unlined face. They were brown like fertile soil, and just as rich with promise. The name Joshua was perfect.

Kainja released Judith's hand and moved toward the boy, dropping to one knee when he was close enough to study the child's face. "It can't be," he said, almost to himself. "I never tasted his blood."

The boy smiled, without pretense or guile. "What can't be, Judas?"

Again Kainja stiffened, at the sound of his name on the boy's lips. "She coached you well," he said. "You are much like him. But I told her. And I tell you. I never drank the blood of Joshua, of the one the Greeks called Jesus Christ. She couldn't have found what wasn't there."

Sister Judith spoke then. Her voice had gained strength. "You never believed, Judas. Even after you became vampire and heard the stories of Jesus risen, you didn't believe. But surely you recall the last supper? The words he gave to each of you?"

In all his centuries, Kainja had never felt as chilled as he did when he remembered what words Judith meant. But in that same instant the cold passed and wonder filled his face, lapping over all the sharp edges of his fragile and terrible beauty. He said the words out loud.

"This is my blood. Take it and drink."

"Now do you understand?" Judith asked. "Across two thousand years, you carried the seeds of the second coming."

Kainja bowed his head; the boy laid a hand on his shoulder and softly spoke: "Forgive me, Judas. For all you've suffered. And for all you *will* suffer, in my name."

Kainja's tongue had deserted him. He couldn't talk. But there was enough strength in him to nod. That was all either of them needed.

VI.

Later, after Joshua slept, Kainja came back to Judith. He knelt by the bed. They both knew what he was offering. They both knew she would reject it.

"I wouldn't make a good vampire," she said. "And I don't want to live forever."

Kainja nodded. Then he took Judith's hand and slipped the wedding band from her finger where it hung loose against the skin. He put it on his own finger—while the woman watched, puzzled.

"We've created a son together," he explained. "The meaning of this ring has changed. You're *my* wife now." He leaned forward to let his mouth glide softly down against Judith's. Her lips were awkward, unskilled, but pliant. A moment passed; Kainja pulled back.

"The ring will be become my pledge," he said. "To Joshua. But mostly to you." He grinned. "The vampire and his lady."

Judith laughed, and the sound was lovely. Kainja kissed her again, longer, his cold lips heating against hers. This time she was the one who pulled back.

"I can't," she whispered. "Even if I'm free to, I can't. There's nothing left of me physically to give."

Kainja shook his head as if to tell her how wrong she was. He touched a thumb to the sharpest of his teeth, brought it out with a tiny opal bead of venom clinging to the tip.

"For an hour," he said. "For all our sakes."

Judith stared at him, then closed her eyes and nodded. "For an hour," she agreed.

Kainja looked at the woman's shuttered lids and smiled. Of this, she was afraid. Though she'd been brave in so many other ways. He stroked her throat with his thumb, smeared his venom in a silken veil across the arteries that fed her brain. He saw her back arch as the rapture began to spread, felt her pulse stagger and then steady. When she opened her eyes again there was a deep, faint light within them.

"Two hours," she said with a grin.

Kainja nodded and pulled away his clothes, slid beneath the sheets to rest his steady chill against her failing warmth. His mouth found the smallness of her breasts, the hardness of her belly. His hand searched lower, toward a greater heat. After a while, she murmured "now" into his caress. Kainja fitted himself to her, into her. And for a time he fed someone else's hunger. Until Judith cried out with an ancient sound and drifted off to sleep wrapped in all the textures of his embrace.

Kainja lay awake in the dark, listening as the life of the woman he loved ebbed away.

VII.

Later on that morning, Sister Judith died, leaving Kainja alone in the Holy Land with the boy called Joshua. Already, the vampire could sense the forces of ruin gathering against them. The last war was coming, but he was ready for the fight.

For Joshua.

For Judith.

For himself.

Author's End Note: Some of you may have seen a movie called Dracula 2000, *in which Dracula is revealed to be Judas Iscariot. I was a bit upset when I first found that out. Kainja is, of course, Judas, but I first wrote of him in 1993, well before* Dracula 2000 *used the same basic idea. I doubt the writer for that movie had ever read my Kainja stories, which appeared in the anthology series* Prisoners of the Night, *but I* knew *I'd gotten there first. Later, it turned out I was wrong and that there were others long before me who connected Judas with vampires. I didn't know that when I first wrote these stories.*

JUDAS NAILED
HIS MOUTH OPEN

With prayers unanswered and wine grown cold
Judas nailed his mouth open with screams
in a stone petaled darksmare
fed with worms

On a nocturnal crucifix of hate
his limbs crossed and shattered
by the scouring teeth of saints
Judas nailed wide his lips and tongue

While aching flagellant thoughts
danced in currents on his brow
the ankle whips and bone-skin drums
sounded as spikes to tired wounds

The silver was heavy in his mouth
pouring bitter from his tears
swollen like bad meat in his belly
crusts of old scars were weeping

The bats of his sins took flight
foam at their sweetened lips
thorns in their wings to pierce his ears
and dance in a place all rotten

With rope so strong in sick dead light
Judas hung himself with his mouth open
in shrieking red-tipped pain
but did not die

The teeth of him are old that fed the night.

HOLOCAUST IN ROSARY

wet eyes in a darkness holy shine
carapace of paint
on apostle faces
silk wine on scaled dry throats

comes trailing psalm
crucifix of cold
leper-winter

voices in scripture dance grief
fingers crying on ribbed beads
of ivory

dirge

church awash in chalice roses
blackened petals
no one kneels
incubus mouths shriek prophecy

fingers crawl epistles
mimes in blood
scalpel-words

sick in the light the faces melt
grow halos of prismed spikes

for god

lost

one mouth with fossil tongue
speaks of sweet Christ dying
of holocaust in rosary

Pray

CLOWNS IN THE DARK

There were faint laughters, as of clowns in the dark, and the falling of shadows, like black flakes of snow. There were movements that lived in the corners of his eyes, always gone when he turned his head. He watched for them in the mirror but could not find them. They hid themselves away from the light, hid themselves away from the knife in his hand and the deadness of his face.

She did not hide. Her image on the bed had crushed metal eyes, which were wet and full of dancers. Her mouth was open, smiling; her body was lax, half hidden in black hair and crimson coverlets. He touched her reflection, fingers parachuting like silk over the dark vision. He kissed the glass, tasting the cold with his tongue. And then he turned and killed her.

Eyes howling, she stared at him as she died, as he put a hand to the wound and watched it turn red. He leaned toward her and she arched her body up for him, but he did nothing except to lay a penny on each lid as it finally closed. Her smile closed too, but more swiftly.

Afterward, he put on a pale face made from her powder and paint, and he colored his lips with blood. Then he danced, alone in a room so newly emptied. His eyes in the mirror neither blinked nor teared, and, after a while, he went and drew a purple droplet just below each lash with her eyeliner. When even that was not enough to reflect his sorrow, he left the house and walked out into rain. Tears ran down his cheeks then, though they tasted of powder not salt, and were cold instead of hot.

He walked in the hiss of mist and pain while carnivals played in his head—rats following—and the tears washed his clown face away. An awning caught him in its shadow and he drifted to a stop there, a dog with him. It came, wet and shivering, and sniffed at his pockets as if hungry. He was hungry too, but he let it lick his fingers. After a time it went away, both the dog and the hunger. The latter for only a little while.

He waited beneath the awning until the rain faded and then followed shining streets back to the house. The bedroom was just as he had left it. The woman was dead. Though, for a moment in the mirror he thought he saw her breast rise in a sigh. She was still empty when he looked straight at her.

He walked a cat-scratched chair up beside the bed on its clawed feet and sat there, taking her hand, no longer afraid to touch and hold her. Her flesh was not really cold and her fingers were only a little stiff. He sat there with her as quietly as he could.

The rain found the city again, bringing down lightning and wind. The wind pushed electric wires together with gleeful spite and a cyan flash photographed the sky. The lights in the house flickered and went cold. In that flicker, he saw that the blood had dried and blackened and was rusting on the sheets. Her hand dropped from his grasp as he fell back against the cushion of the chair. This time the tears were real.

Morning came empty handed and he had not slept. With eyes burning red from seeing, he left that place, bird song hollow in his ears. The collar of a coat covered his face, though not because of the cold. The knife, on a thong around his neck, hung down between his nipples and hardened each in turn with its swinging caress. And the rats and other things followed with quick skittering steps.

The sounds of people—of buses, of horns, and of slamming doors—drove nails through his head, and the hunger in him was an animal with its paw in a trap. But when he walked past the stalls of the market he found the sight of food nauseating and turned aside.

By evening he had returned once more to the house, blown, perhaps, by an east wind that held iced razors in its grasp. He did not really want to go in. But he needed to. The skin on his body began to writhe, twisting itself into knots. He moaned deep in his throat. A hand went out of its own volition and he caught it and drove it back to his side.

Somewhere, some thing played with fingernails on a chalkboard harp, and a gust of wind flapped cold wings by and spat drizzle down his neck. There were eyes in the walls watching, and fingers beckoning that he could not refuse. He shivered and took hold of the latch. It grabbed at him and the door swung open without his wish. Someone was there, someone alive who smelled strongly of sheared copper and musk, someone who chuckled in a voice that resonated just below his auditory threshold. He jerked his hand free from the door and lurched away.

That first backward movement became a flood of running—down alleys that lengthened constantly into distance, past garbage cans that fanged his ankles—running, to any place but the place where he was, running, though he knew he would be followed. A sign stopped him at last, knocking him down as he ran into it. He lay beneath it while his heart counted the seconds, then rolled over and got to his feet. The sign hung white in his eyes.

"Welcome Home," it read.

He glanced up to see the steeple of a church rising over him, soaring up into a sky that flickered like an empty channel on a television set. A corner of the church that was framed on two sides by uncut stone seemed to beckon him, and he went over and huddled in its jaws.

He tried to pray, as he had done in childhood, but the words had long since fossilized in his mouth. "Blood of Christ" was all he could remember, and he kept repeating it while the rats and strange dancers came to caper about him and call him names for his impotence. They were never there when he looked for them, though he felt their teeth.

He drew the knife up over his head and fingered it, crouching like one of the churchyard shrubs while he watched the streets twist away like snakes from the running cups of his eyes. At each sound of footsteps, he started.

Yet, he did not hear her when she came, did not know she was there until her nails touched his cheek and he leaped to his feet. He could not run, pinned as he was by the owl-swift turn of her head. She smiled, and worms crawled there, and there were angels in her eyes with fatal wings spread. All her wounds had puckered and pearled. He could not even see where his knife had gone in through the throat.

The fingers left his face and slid down his shoulder toward the knife, leaving furrows of red behind. She took away the blade and he offered no resistance.

"Why do you run?" she asked. "You know I will have you."

"I don't like to kill…. You," he said.

She laughed at that and brought her mouth down on his. Her nails ran up under his shirt and sliced through his nipples. Her teeth ripped his lips, bringing blood. Nerves stood out under his skin, orchestrating stillborn shrieks as her sandpaper touch rubbed them raw.

When she pulled back, a white vapor that came from him hung for a moment in the sky between them before it was pulled in like smoke through her nostrils. Her pupils rolled up and she softened against him. Then her body bucked under his hands and he held her tight to keep her from falling.

She opened her eyes wide and smiled. "Another piece of your soul," she said, and tongued her teeth.

The rats, her things, her familiars, repeated her words, as if he had not heard her. He could almost see them now, capering about on broken legs with hempen ropes around their necks. He could certainly feel them crawling beneath the skin of his chest. He could feel their incisors tickling up his spine. He could….

"You must be hungry," the woman said, pushing away from him.

The rats giggled and told him with glee how many she had

done this to before, how many she had fed until they were glutted with her, and how many she had eaten the souls from as if they were cabbages. He closed his eyes. The rats were gone and he had not yet answered her.

"Speak," she hissed, tongue whipping from between her lips. "Tell me. Now!"

"I hunger," he said, his voice like a burning tree. "God help me, I hunger."

"Then feed," she said. "But do not waste it this time."

She took the knife that he had carried and drove it upward into her lungs. Her eyes shuttered and a smile emptied her face.

Leaving the knife buried, she reached a bloody hand up to his lips. He licked her fingers, as the dog had licked his the night before. The blood ran dark against the bone color of her skin, so lovely a contrast.

He went down to his knees, holding her body with his hands while her life fell down on his face and he opened his mouth to taste the salty heat of it. He drank long, until his hunger was appeased, until she died the death from which she would awaken again, and again, and again, forever. His soul would not last nearly so long.

* * * * * * *

His face in the mirror was pale as frost, a harlequin's face drawn with powdered chalk around dark eyes. But he had put the smile on backwards.

NIGHT FALL

They stepped out of the plane together, knowing it was a long way to fall. And at first Melissa was afraid. It wasn't because she had never done this before. She had parachuted many times, but never in darkness, and never for the reason she was doing it tonight.

She looked at Julian Martel across a distance of inches, and the moon was so gorged with light that she could read every sharp edge and angle of his face. It was hard for her to believe that this glorious Italian was strapped to her in a tandem parachute, and that they would make love tonight as they floated down to Earth through vast and silvered cloudscapes.

She wondered for a moment how she'd let Julian talk her into this. But, when the oversized parachute blossomed overhead and she saw Julian smile and heard him whisper her pet name, "Lissa," she knew. Since they had first met—only three weeks before—she'd agreed to anything and everything he asked, even to this, even to making love in a double harness while they dropped ten thousand feet. That height would give them about twenty minutes.

Though they had been together only three times before, Melissa had always known Julian as an unrushed and patient lover. Even now, even with such a short time, he did not hurry. She wore a body suit, with snaps between the legs, and over it she'd thrown an extra-large coverall that Julian easily unzipped and pushed away from her hips. He wore only a pair of shorts and a T-shirt.

Though the wind was cold, Julian didn't seem to mind, and in another minute Melissa forgot the temperature of the air herself as her lover's mouth found hers, and his body found hers. She arched herself for him, freeing her knees from encumbering cloth, and he was with her, inside where a furnace had stoked itself to a lava heat in readiness.

The explosion of her release was soundless when it came, though Melissa's mouth was open wide, drying in the rush of wind, and Julian's mouth was buried at the base of her throat as if his lips could draw the essence of her out through her skin. It ached, there below her chin, there between her legs, and in her chest where her heart pounded and pounded. It ached and she didn't mind.

"Lissa," she heard. A whisper. And a quilt-like softness settled over her limbs, over her eyes and over her heart. She had never felt so empty and so filled at the same time.

Her eyes closed and her head drifted forward onto Julian's shoulder. His skin, normally so satin-cool, had bloomed with a coal-fire warmth. It was like that when they finished love, as if he drew heat from her and banked it inside his own flesh. Melissa stroked her lover's arm as it went tightly about her waist and pulled her into that warmth, and above her head in the night sky she heard a twanging sound.

Then she heard it again.

The silk of their canopy spilled air and they dropped a few feet with jaw tightening swiftness. Melissa's contentment vanished as the harness of the parachute drew ligatures about her shoulders and upper body. She looked up in panic, and saw Julian's thumb and forefinger encircle one of the suspension lines and snap it with a flick of fingernails. His palm opened afterward, and in the moonlight it looked as if he wore a glove of thorns.

Melissa screamed, "no," as Julian's hand suddenly sliced back and forth above their heads and left them with nothing but air for support. She grabbed at him with desperate, insane tightness, but the increasing rip of the wind tore them apart an instant later. She saw Julian clearly for just one more moment, saw his white face and his dark smile clotted with red. She saw his T-shirt split open as his shoulders bulged from within. Then she saw the wings unfold. A stroke of those wings caught the air and Julian's descent was halted. Melissa went past him, watched his lips fill up with her name as she reached out, and hit the ground.

* * * * * * *

Lissa did not know how long it was before she came to. Julian knelt beside her, holding her head and giving her a drink that tasted of salt and warmth. She pushed him away and climbed to her feet.

Her body was whole when she looked down at herself, though she felt so light that she almost believed she could fly. Julian seemed normal too. Had she only imagined wings sprouting from his back?

"I'm alive," she said, in wonder.

Julian stepped forward, and just for a moment let her see his face as it really was.

"No you're not," he said.

MESSIAH

First Prologue

Where the prophet knelt, the stones of the Negev desert ran with blood, blood from lacerated knees and from hands and feet, and from his forehead where it kissed sand. It ran steadily, like the dry rasp of his voice lifted up in prayer. He ignored it.

But he could not ignore the rising sun, and the fraction of heat that touched him was enough to lift his head. The face was pale, skin drawn parchment tight over hollowed cheekbones. The eyes were the color of desert pavement. He stood and walked into the cave at his back.

I.

An old woman led the penitents, and it was her will alone that kept them moving on across the sands. It was her chant that paid homage to the sun, and it was her voice that kept their eyes fixed on a faint line of white hills gleaming like a promise ahead. At dusk the promise was fulfilled.

The woman squatted before one cave among many. The others joined her, licking dry lips that had cracked in the sun. It was full dark within minutes and the watchers stirred with questions.

"He is a holy one?" someone asked.

"Perhaps," said the woman. "A prophet at the least."

A third spoke then, a Cyrenian known as John. "It is said that he saw the Christ, that he came on the day of crucifixion when it was dark from the sixth to the ninth hour and the temple veil was torn."

"I too have heard that," the woman said. "But I do not know if it is true. If we but wait a moment longer we may have our answer."

Second Prologue

He rose up through crimson dreams to wakefulness, rising up to the night that breathed softly outside his cavern home. The dreams were no longer of him and he scattered them away. At last, his face composed, he strode out into the darkness.

II.

The penitents could scarcely see the prophet where he stood in the shadow of the cave, and it was as if he did not see them at all. He knelt and bowed his head to the rock, and began to pray.

No one spoke for an hour. And then, "water," someone said. It was a small interruption but enough to make the prophet look up. He knelt back on his heels, hands hidden within the sleeves of his linen garment, the only clothing that he wore. His hair hung long and unwashed and there was blood on his forehead.

"What do you want of me?" he asked them.

It was the old woman who spoke. "We have heard that you saw the Christ," she said. "We would know the truth of it."

"I saw him," the prophet said.

The crowd leaned forward at his speech, as if to drag words from his mouth. "Tell us," came from a dozen throats.

"I saw him three times," the prophet said. "Once in Gethsemane when he wept blood tears, again when he spoke that night before the high priest, and last when he was dead on the cross."

"What of him can you offer us?" John the Cyrenian asked."

The prophet lowered his head. His voice was weak in reply. "I have nothing of him that I can share," he said.

The crowd felt itself destroyed by those words. Sometimes it was hard to tell the prophets from the imbeciles who muttered to themselves in the street. But this one had seen Christ! They had thought him a prophet; now they thought him a fool. And they were unforgiving of fools. One threw a crust of bread, a second blasphemed. A third laughed at the old woman, including her among the simple.

The prophet grew angry for the woman, who did not flinch. "Enough," he shouted. "Did you learn nothing from Jesus? You want no truth. You want a show, a drama. That I can give you."

With his last words the prophet stood and rent his garments, and the crowd could not believe when they saw him began to change. His hands were suddenly free of the constraints of his sleeves and their nails were long and dead white. Brown eyes turned furnace yellow, and the skin on his face grew sunken like that of a corpse. And there were blood marks on his head and body, on his hands and feet, and wetness ran down his left side beneath the garment. The marks were of thorns and nails and of a spear.

"The stigmata of Christ," breathed the old woman.

The crowd only ran as a voice mocked them. "Let he who doubts put his hand to my wounds."

A few looked back, and never forgot. The prophet's feet did not touch the ground and golden motes of dust spun madly around him. Those who had looked back ran harder, and the night was soon empty except for the old woman and the prophet.

The woman had closed her eyes but she opened them now. The prophet sat quietly on the stone, his face once more human and his hands inside his sleeves. She went to him, and only as she got closer did she see that he was weeping.

She touched his shoulder. He looked up.

"Who are you?" she asked. "You are not He?"

"No," said the prophet tiredly. "I am not even fit to carry his wounds."

"Then how do you?"

"Because. On Golgotha, beneath the cross, I tasted a drop of Christ's blood. It was on the wood where it had run down from the spear in his side. That drop nearly killed, but in the end it healed. When I knew myself again I carried the stigmata you see. But I did not hunger. I did not hunger and I did not hunt! I came here to give him thanks. But it is so hard to be a saint. Can you understand that?"

"No," she said. "I do not understand. To bear the marks of Christ is a wondrous gift. One that I have begged for myself."

"Would that I could pass its burden on to you," the vampire said, looking down.

The woman nodded to herself as she drew a sharp silver dagger from beneath her robe.

"You will," she said. "When I drink your blood."

TWISTED LITTLE THING

Twisted little thing
Darling snake-eyed witch
Wasted strutter in black silk
Burned my heart
Made me like it
When she licked my tears
Away

WET ACID ANGEL

Wet acid angel,
trapped in a black haze
of ghostly desire

Scarlet nailed witch
with eyes of white longing
and touch-swollen lips

Shade me with your
cross of need,
love my mouth,
taste my nighted tongue

Bleed to me
in heated red
delight.

LOVE IN THE
TIME OF CYBERSEX

In the late twentieth century came the internet. From the internet was born "Chat." And Chat led to cybering, to online sex between parties who sat at home in their comfortable chairs and typed reciprocal erotica and porn to each other on their computers.

In the early twenty-first century Chat became virtual reality. Chatters plugged directly into their HEVE—home electronic video entertainment interface—created characters from the data streams, and inhabited virtual bodies in a virtual world. The online sex was better. Sometimes when people were locked virtual skin to virtual skin they could almost forget that they weren't actually exchanging bodily fluids.

By the mid twenty-first century, mundane reality was still boring but virtual reality was no longer good enough.

—from "Sex: The New Story of an Old Act."

There were two vampires, a shapeshifter in semi-human form, a sword-witch, a demon named Baell, and a dozen sluts of various persuasions and genders on the battlements when Boone came on. And the low sky was like ice from the vac-shield, a half solid, shifting weave of thin light that kept the black of space away from the surface of the Sea of Tranquility. Trapped beneath the shield lay a bubble of oxygen, and above it gleamed the stars. Always the stars. From the roof of the lunar dome, built like the keep of an ancient castle, those distant suns could have been the jeweled eyes of gods in a forest so given over to night that you couldn't see the trees.

Beneath the terrible stars, the vampires were fucking the witch.

Boone ignored the three-way cyber and found a corner where he could lean and watch those who watched him. He'd already slipped fully into his barbarian persona. Each time he'd awakened from the sleep that was still a necessity even on vacation, he'd found it easier. He wondered how long it would take to forget that he wasn't really 6' 4" and 275, that he couldn't bend horseshoes with his real hands and that in his own body he'd never killed anyone with a black axe like the one hanging now over his right shoulder.

Some people could probably afford vacations long enough to learn to forget, but this was Boone's last night. In the morning he'd find himself back on Earth, in his own head, in the persona booth delivered to his bedroom seven days ago by the travel agent for Cyberworld Adventures.

But before he went—

The shapeshifter prowled toward him, as if her bones and muscles weren't quite human. And they weren't. Persona vats could grow anything. He'd seen a dragon here last night for sweet sake, though the cost of downloading one's mind into something like that was astronomically high. But the shifter body was almost standard, and with practice the person inhabiting it could make it change shape. In the lighter gravity of the moon, the werewolf myth could come howling to life.

This shifter was named Smokeheart, a werepanther instead of a wolf, and she hadn't been here quite long enough to learn how to fully control her body. She remained mostly human, except for pointed and tufted ears and a rampant grace, and a tail as strong and flexible as satin rope. Boone recalled that tail fondly.

"Greets, Kain," Smokeheart said, using Boone's cyber-name. "How is our axe-wielding barbarian this eve?"

Boone/Kain felt his lips curve, felt shadows drip from the

corners of his mouth as he answered in a voice that seemed odd to his ears even though its deep roughness fitted naturally with the bladed scars on the face he currently wore.

"Doing well, Smoke. "You not hanging with the vamps tonight?"

He gestured across the 'ments to where the two male vampires had the sword-witch sandwiched between them, their shafts buried in her body while their fangs were buried in her shoulders and throat.

Smoke laughed. "Even one night would have been too much. I never cared much for vampires. They're not brothers, you know."

Kain shrugged. "Not even blood brothers?" he asked jokingly. "They look alike." And they did, both with pale flesh and blond hair that nearly matched their dusters of ivory leather.

Again Smoke laughed, and leaned closer to whisper. "They're sisters. Wanted to know what it was like to fuck like males." She shook her head with a sinuous motion that made parts of Kain's body throb. "Personally, I think they've got problems. But I guess we all do."

Kain repeated his shrug.

From behind him in the deepest shadows of the battlements came a low trembling growl and the hiss of friction as other bodies mated—furred bodies. The ones who were shyer than the vamps usually did it in the dark, or in the rooms below in the dome. The barbarian didn't look. Smokeheart did, and smirked. She sniffed the air.

"Werewolves," she said. "Cute. But they smell like wet dogs." And then: "I suppose you're waiting for her?"

Kain glanced at the shifter, gave a half smile and reached out to finger-stroke her sharp-pointed chin. "I have to."

"You want to."

"Yeah."

Smoke nodded, her green eyes flickering and inscrutable, like the waltz of fireflies over dark water.

"Then I'll warn you," she said. "Baell wants her, too. I heard him telling it around. Said an angel deserved a demon on her last night."

Kain's teeth clenched; his jaw muscles twitched. He did not like Baell. The two had already clashed wits on the battlements, though no blows had yet fallen. That might change tonight.

Smokeheart was turning away and Kain started to murmur a "thank you" for her warning when a woman came on the 'ments. *The* woman. The one he had waited for. She *was* an angel. Literally.

Her hair was golden white, falling to her heels in a weave of silken tangles. Her skin was lighter than her hair, and as translucent as you would expect an angel's flesh to be. Even whiter were her wings, though whitest of all was the spirit that animated her.

Kain shivered. For six evenings he had watched this woman leave the battlements with a different man, just as he had left with a different lady. But not *this* evening.

He started toward her, forgetting that he was a barbarian warrior and should stalk like a conquering hero. In that moment he was only Boone—in awe. But before he could reach her, someone else stepped in the way. It was Baell, Baell who was bowing from the waist, who was kissing the angel's hand and murmuring with a silken tongue:

"My lady. Surely on your final night you will grant this poor devil a dance...or two."

And Boone/Kain stepped around the demon's huge shoulder, and shook the long hair back from his yellow-brown eyes.

"But the last dance is mine," he said.

The angel's name was Miramia. She turned from Baell to Kain, her cut-diamond eyes as clear and bright as sun-burnished shields. The demon turned too, his leathery wings snapping and fluttering in the air. His inky mouth sneered from a scarlet face. But Kain ignored the sneer, gazed only into the scintillant eyes of the woman, and at her lips where they were parted and gleaming.

"You seem very sure of yourself, warrior," Miramia said. Her voice was sweet and rich as the ringing of silver chimes on an ensorcelled night, and yet there was restraint in her words. "The choice of last dance is mine to make."

Kain inclined his head. "The choice is yours. Certainly. And I am not sure of myself. But I have faith. And what more does one need to win a moment with an angel."

Miramia laughed and clapped her hands. She was barely five feet tall and her wings arched above her head like snowy flames.

"Excellent," she said.

Kain smiled, and Baell hit him from his blind side.

If he'd truly been a barbarian, Kain might have been expecting that blow. As it was, the slam of the demon's fist spun him halfway around and sent him stumbling to one knee. Someone screamed. Baell was over seven feet tall, would have weighed maybe four hundred pounds on Earth. Even on the moon he had the strength that such mass gave him.

Kain started to rise and was struck again by the chop of a huge hand across his neck. He went down on his face, his heart drumming a frenzy, and before he could even think of rolling over a hard-nailed foot slammed into his ribs, sent him tumbling over the stone flaggings.

He came up with a roar, grabbing for his axe, but Baell was running with Miramia clutched against his chest. The angel snarled, fought, but Baell was more than twice her size. And then the demon launched them both over the four foot wall that girded the battlements, his broad wings skimming the reaching stone as Miramia cried out. Captor and captive dropped from sight.

Kain raced after. At the wall he met Smokeheart. And far below on the stark lunar plain, Baell glided to a landing with a limp white bundle in his arms.

"He hit her, too, the bastard," Smoke said. "Just as they went over. I think she's dazed."

Kain pulled himself up on the crenelated wall as Baell ran off into the gloom of the Sea of Tranquility.

"I'm with you," Smokeheart growled. "The monitors won't stop this. They'll treat it as role-play."

Kain glanced at the shifter for only an instant. "Mine to win. Or to lose," he said. And he dropped over the wall.

It was over forty feet down from the top of the 'ments to the top of the lunar dome on which it stood. Even in one-sixth Earth gravity Kain hit hard, his legs buckling so that he fell backward, crying out with the pain of shocked limbs and muscles, crying out more as a civilized man named Boone than as a barbarian called Kain.

But he barely had time to register pain before he was sliding down the long curve of the dome toward the moon's surface, picking up speed as he went. His hands slapped against plasti-glass, clutching for support. There wasn't any.

Faster now. And faster! Panic burned in his throat. If he couldn't slow down— If he started to tumble— It would kill him to hit the ground. What was he doing here? He was no barbarian. No hero. He taught school, for sweet sake.

A flash of memory sliced his mind like a scalpel. A vid-tape he'd seen. The colony children sometimes "rode the dome" for fun.

Maybe....

Kain was on his side but managed to twist himself over onto his back, nearly throwing himself into a roll before he got his knees up and his hobnailed boots pushed down against the curve of the glass. His hands pressed down hard and he began to use the friction of palms and heels to slow and guide him.

It couldn't have been done on earth, but when Kain came sprawling off the edge of the structure into the thick dust of the moon's surface, he was alive and without any broken bones. His palms burned from the friction of the glass, but he ignored that pain and staggered up, sneezing at the fine gray powder that coated him.

There was no sign of Baell and Miramia. But there would be tracks, he thought. Then he realized, there were thousands of them. Once there had been only two sets of boot prints on the Sea of Tranquility, but the Mare was shielded now and oxygen had been pumped in for those who wanted to explore or play amid the "magnificent desolation." Kain was no hunter to find one set of tracks among many.

A screech of claws on plastiglass brought Kain's head around and he saw that Smokeheart hadn't listened to his "mine to win or lose" speech. She'd discarded her clothes and was morphing into her "were" form. Her trip down the dome had gone easier than his.

"Don't argue," were the first words from the shifter's mouth. "You'll never find Baell's tracks among all the others. But I can smell him. He can still be your meat when we catch up."

She didn't wait for an answer but took off across the plain, her body continuing to ripple and change until she flowed over stones and dust as a panther with a coat as black as a vacuum sky. Kain followed, struggling to keep up even though each stride carried him a dozen feet.

Dust rose, fell so slowly that they were yards away before it settled. At a glance there seemed few places to hide upon the rock strewn landscape. That discounted the rich harvest of craters dotting the Mare. At the wall of one such crater, Smokeheart came slinking to a stop. Kain joined her, and below stood the demon Baell facing off with an angel whose pale gown floated half-torn around her.

Miramia wasn't dazed any longer. Her wings throbbed with anger; her fists were clenched. Baell grabbed her by the arm and she punched him flat in the face. The demon roared and punched her back, sent her reeling to the ground. She rose, her body a gleaming brand of silver-white beneath the earthshine.

Smokeheart snarled from beside Kain, looked at the barbarian with emerald eyes that shredded like talons.

"Take him!" she said. "If you fail, I won't."

But Kain had already risen to his feet.

"Baell!" he shouted.

The demon looked up, and Kain saw the rage that curved the being's ebon lips.

"She's mine, Barbarian! Go now and I won't have to maim you."

Kain laughed, strode down the curved wall of the crater as if striding into an arena. In that moment he *was* a barbarian.

"Come and make me," he said.

Baell smirked, and drew from over his back, from between his wings, a heavy mace of dark iron with scarlet spikes adorning it.

"You know what they call these things, don't you, hero?" Baell snapped as he strode across the crater floor. "They call them sword-breakers."

"That's why I brought an axe," Kain said, as he pulled the black steel of his own weapon over his shoulder.

Baell shook his head, and leaped to bring his mace down with a shout of, "kill you!"

Kain blocked the blow on the haft of his axe. Iron clanged on steel. Both weapons shivered in the still air.

The back of Kain's axe had a hook forged to snare enemy blades. He tried to use it to tear away Baell's mace. But the demon was too smart or too quick to let that happen. He twisted the spiked club away, then lashed out with a taloned foot that raked through the leather of Kain's breeks and brought blood welling from the barbarian's left thigh.

It was Kain's turn to snarl. He lashed a backhand blow at Baell. The demon leaped aside and Kain spun, brought his axe crashing down. Axe met mace. Sparks sleeted. For a moment the two stood face to face, weapons locked, arms and shoulders and chests straining until—with a surge of bulging muscles— Baell threw the smaller warrior back against the rough crater wall.

Kain realized he could never match the demon's strength. Baell realized the same thing at the same time and dropped his mace to grapple with the barbarian. One huge hand caught the haft of Kain's battle-axe just below the blade and forced it back against stone; the other hand found Kain's throat and clamped tight.

Kain struggled to drag his axe forward while his left hand clutched at the demon's wrist, clawing and tearing in an effort to break the choke-hold. Baell only redoubled his efforts, bearing down savagely with his scarlet face contorted in fury and his black fingernails digging into Kain's flesh.

Jagged floaters serrated Kain's vision. He tasted blood from where he'd bitten his tongue, and tasted fear like the stroke of an electric whip. If you died in persona you could die forever. Or if you survived you might wake screaming from nightmares the rest of your days. It was the cost of making games real.

Kain dropped his weapon, punched the demon in the jaw once, twice. Baell only shook his head, smashed back with a knotted fist again and again into the shorter man's face.

Kain's lips split. Blood sprayed. He could hear his heart pounding, pounding. Then he heard something else, a low growl that he barely recognized as coming from his own throat.

With rage arcing through ever muscle in his body, he twisted free of Baell's grip and ducked under a swing, then threw himself forward to wrap both arms around his enemy's waist. With legs churning, he picked the demon up and carried him back a dozen steps before slamming him into the ground. But Baell was ready for that and even as he went down he grabbed Kain's wrists and flipped the barbarian over his head.

Kain landed hard, tried to roll over with his lungs grabbing for air that had fled. He got to his knees, and the earth's light was suddenly blotted out as the demon came swooping, crimson wings spread wide. There was no time to avoid the blow.

Baell struck with his entire body, with skull and shoulders and chest, and with an elbow that snapped the barbarian's head back. Kain felt a shock tear along his spine and for an instant his legs went liquid and lost. And he was down, with the demon laughing madly astride his chest. He saw Baell pull a triangular dagger from a belt sash, saw it rise with a glimmer of silver-blue light along it.

He heard, also, the rattle of rocks and a distant growling cry, and he knew Smokeheart was coming fast down the crater wall. But he also knew she was going to be too late. Baell's lips writhed with hate and glee; the dagger was poised to fall.

"Smokeheart!" Kain shouted. "Get Miramia out of here!" He spat in Baell's face.

The demon roared, scarlet knuckles going white with strain as the knife ripped downward. That stroke never landed. The knife went flying, in slow motion, and in the same extended motion the demon's body toppled sideways into the dirt.

Above where Kain and Baell had fought stood Miramia, her eyes flinty and polar-cold as she held the demon's mace in her small fists. The iron of it dripped with blood.

"Looked like you needed help," the angel said.

Kain spat a glob of bright red phlegm into the lunar dust. "That I did."

He tried to move, found with some surprise that he could, though his back twinged and pins and needles stabbed his legs. He gave a wince, and Smokeheart was there in human form to grasp his shoulder and help him rise. Miramia came to help as well, tossing the mace down with a thud.

Kain looked from one woman to the other. Smokeheart smiled, like a fresh rush of birdsong, but the smile slid, melted into some alloy of fondness and melancholy. The shifter nodded into the barbarian's gaze and turned away. Kain watched her slip smoothly into her panther form and disappear up the side of the crater. He sighed, glanced toward Miramia, who studied him with an enigmatic frown.

"What is it you want of me?" the angel asked.

Kain considered a dozen responses that he'd practiced for just such a question, and discarded them all.

"Just you," he said. "I just want you."

"Why?"

"Because," he gestured around at the dust and the sharp shadows, and at the body of Baell lying still before them, "none of this is real. But you're real. Not the visual. Not the wings. The inside. The hidden."

Miramia's diamond gaze was like a laser cutting into his. For an eon she dissected him. But she asked no further questions, made no further comment. Instead, she reached and caught his fingers, and a little tug brought him along in her wake as she turned and strode away.

Up onto the floor of the Sea of Tranquility they went, and although it was growing late on their last day they did not hurry. A mile further into the desolation they came to a place where many lovers had come before. It was a massive conservatory, filled with thousands of species of rare plants and animals, built both for tourists and for colonists, and as insurance against the extinction of such species on the home world.

Much of the building was underground, but there were glass rooms beneath the earth-shine where Honeycreepers and Birds of Paradise and Ivory Billed Woodpeckers flitted and called and courted amid the blooms of Monkshood and Evening Primrose. It was to one such room that Miramia and Kain went, and the air was soft, redolent with Thornmint and Myrrh, resonant with the purl of streams and the murmur of frogs.

The two found a moss filled cranny where a waterfall misted the air with miniature rainbows. Previous sojourners had left candles and Kain lit them, setting them in stony nooks so that he and the angel were surrounded by firefly lights.

Through the polished glass above them came the actinic bite of the brittle stars, and the mellower blue-silver sheen of the earth as it sank slowly toward the horizon. Kain blotted out the falling planet and the passing of time that it signaled by pulling Miramia down on top of him on the mossy ground. Her wings lifted, expanded, closing out his view like drifts of warm snow.

She straddled him, her hands seeking, finding, loosening the scarlet ties of his leather breeks. His own hands wove into the pale rustle of her gown, drew it up over her knees, and then over her waist. She gasped as his fingers swept the delicate inclines of her thighs, and leaned down toward him to blend her mouth with his. Their tongues warred, and as Miramia broke the kiss she thrust from the hips to link their bodies.

Kain moaned and arched hard into his lover. His hands drifted, caressed silk, drew open the thin film of the angel's dress so that her breasts fell burning into his palms. Miramia raised her upper body, leaned back and plunged downward from the waist, drew away slowly, plunged again. Her feathered wings beat and beat; tension fled her face.

The waterfall whispered and a breeze trembled the ferns. A fog of silver droplets floated across the lovers. Kain shivered, seeing the beads of mist that glistened in Miramia's winter-gold hair. His fingers pinched the cinnamon-coral of the woman's nipples. With a flash of feral teeth she bit at her lower lip. Her hands dropped to Kain's chest, nails curved and digging as she closed her mirror eyes.

Sex locked to sex, they sped their rhythm. And in a dream of heat their bodies tangled, muscles taut as wild poetry beneath skins that had slicked with sweat.

Miramia's wings fluttered, went still, fluttered. The rustle of them filled the hollow where the man and woman coupled, filled it until the sound burst into Kain's ears like the shout of snare drums.

He tensed, groaned.

A parrot startled in a thrash of iridescent plumage.

The barbarian and the angel lunged together, hearts banging against ribs, hips flailing now. Their twinned cries came as echoes, raising a weave of Luna Moths that stormed up from the candle-lit rocks in a tornado of turquoise.

Miramia opened her eyes and smiled, her lower body still moving but that movement grown suddenly languid. Kain panted, reached up to lose his hands in the fall of the angel's hair. He drew her down for a kiss, held that kiss until they both needed breath.

The disk of the earth dropped below the moon's horizon, fading out with a flash of pearl-blue. At that instant the bodies of Kain and Miramia were emptied, their lips just touching.

* * * * * * *

Kain was gone and Boone awoke in his own body, in his own bedroom, in the persona booth on earth. The saline gel that had surrounded and supported him for the past week had already drained away and he'd been dried by warm air currents from the machine in which his flesh had slept. The feeding tubes had also been detached, before he became aware enough to know they were there, and now the last needle retreated from his arm and the booth opened.

For a moment more he lay cradled in the foam cushion at the heart of the big computer, then slid his legs over the side and stood up. He swayed, felt the weirdness of having to readjust to the movements of his natural limbs. His surroundings seemed strange, too, even though he'd spent his nights sleeping in this dark-paneled room for the past year.

He sighed, went out into the hallway and down it, listening to the quiet hush of the early morning house. At a second bedroom he stopped, pushed wide the door and entered. Amid pastel walls and delicate rice paper sketches there squatted—like some alien artifact cobbled together from metal and glass—a second persona booth. It, too, was open, and in it lay his wife. She gave him a half smile as he looked in on her.

He did not *quite* smile back, but leaned into the device to pick her up in his arms. She was not very heavy. Her disease had wasted her away over a decade until her bones pressed tight against almost translucent skin.

He carried her the few steps to the nearby bed and laid her upon it, then sat down beside her. She could still move her head, and she turned it slightly to gaze at him with the pale blue eyes that were as alive as they'd been the day he met her.

"You're an angel," she said, her voice whispering, husky with strain.

Boone ignored the fact that his wife didn't mean her words exactly the way he wanted to hear them.

"We both know who the angel is here," he said.

"I wasn't an angel to Baell when I hit him upside the head with his own mace."

Boone gave a small chuckle. "I'm glad. Else I might not have woken up today."

"And how did you like your vacation?"

"The last part was the best," he said.

She looked down. "I was glad to be whole again for you. To be able to walk and run again."

"I was glad to *see* you walk and run. Because it made you glad. But it wasn't something I had to have for myself."

Again she looked at him, and her words were bitter. "Oh yeah, you want to be chained to a cripple."

"For over a year I've heard you say that. Ever since you decided I was more of a caretaker than a husband to you. But I don't think of you as a cripple. I didn't need to go to the moon to see you as beautiful."

Her cheek jumped as if she were angry.

"How can you be a husband when I can't be a wife," she said.

But then the first tears rolled. And others followed until she turned her face to the pillow, crying without sobbing, crying quietly.

"Shhh," he said, not knowing what else to say. He slid down on the bed beside her and put his arms around her. "Shhh," he said again. And: "Like I told Miramia, I just want you. Just you. My wife. Amy."

Amy's arm trembled and Boone knew she was trying to lift it. He caught her fingers in his, drew her bird-like hand up to nuzzle it gently.

"I wish I could touch you," she whispered.

Boone heard the frustration in his wife's voice, and the self-loathing. And he tried one more time to convince her that the constraints of her illness didn't matter to him.

"You *do* touch me," he said. "For all our years. Like no other."

Her voice when it came was even smaller than usual. "And what of Kain's women? The ones you had before the angel? In your nights as a barbarian?"

"None of them were you," he said.

A minute passed, and another before she spoke. "I wanted you to be free," she said. "For a little while. It's been a long few years for you."

He kissed her nose. "It was fun playing someone else. Like being a kid again. But I'm not really a kid. A *man* needs a woman, and the form of the woman isn't as important as how much she loves him."

"Maybe I don't even know how to love anymore. Maybe the disease took that, too."

"Nope. Less than hour ago I felt it in you. We both did. Under the disk of the earth as it set."

Amy had stopped crying but her eyes still brimmed.

"I do love you," she whispered finally. "I only wish...."

"How long do you have to wish for what you can't have before you start to wish for what you can?"

His words sounded harsher than he'd intended and he half expected her to cry again. She didn't. Instead, the right side of her mouth quirked up in the little smile that he'd always adored on her but which he'd seldom seen these past years.

Her glance met his, seemed to bounce back as some deeper thought surfaced behind her blue irises. "The choice of last dance is mine to make," she said softly, repeating something she'd said to him as Miramia. This time it held a different meaning.

"The choice *is* yours," he replied. "And I have faith that you'll remember what's always been inside of you. Let me move back into our bedroom. Let's discover how to be together again." He paused for a slow beat before grinning at her. "It's hard living in the house with a gorgeous woman and not being able to have my evil way with her."

She smirked. "I suppose you'll want me to just lay here."

He grinned hugely. "Ooh, baby. You know what I like."

She grinned too, suddenly, without thinking of anything but how good it felt to be cherished.

"You *are* an angel." she said, and this time she meant it just the way Boone wanted to hear it.

But then she looked at him with that familiar quirk to the side of her mouth again.

"You did lie to me about one thing," she said.

He raised his eyebrows. "What?"

"The women Kain slept with.... You lied about those. Or about one of them at least."

He frowned. "I have no idea what you're talking about."

"None of them was me, you said. Well, I arranged a little adventure for myself without mentioning it to you. A little surprise for us both. Some people on the chat play more than one character, you know. Tell me, what did you think of Smokeheart's tail?"

Boone looked at his wife with astonishment and then laughed out loud before kissing her. She was already clad in white, and even without her wings they found a way to make love.

THE POETRY OF BLOOD

The poet dips his quill in a tiny puddle of iron-black ink and brushes a delicate calligraphy across the pale swath of his manuscript, each stroke delivered as precisely as that of a surgeon with a scalpel. His lips move as he reads his own words.

"I dream in midnight claret, my mouth torn with sorrow."

The manuscript does not speak, can not around the satin gag that binds her mouth. But now she allows herself to breathe, allows her chest to rise and fall beneath the wealth of fine dark lines that etch her arms and legs, her belly and one of her breasts. And her eyes are expressive, wet with a holy shine that the poet kisses lightly away.

"Not much more," the poet says kindly. "A few haikus worth, perhaps."

He soothes the manuscript's damp brow with a sandpaper-dry palm, then leans back in his chair beside the bed where his canvas lies in chains and picks up the smallest and sharpest of his knives. The manuscript shudders, but the poet only trims his quill to a fresh sharpness and returns the blade to its defined space on his bedside worktable. Once again he dips quill to ink; once again he writes and reads.

"I dream in white and ebon, dressed as a harlequin in shards of poetry. And my tongue is that of wolves."

He has chosen the manuscript's remaining breast for these words, and as if from the dark inscriptions themselves an electric scent arises. It is composed of adrenaline and pheromones and clings to the delicate textures beneath. The poet leans forward before it can dissipate to draw it into his lungs through his nostrils. His mouth lingers close to the source of the scent; his tongue caresses the nipple to draw a last bead of musk into his mouth. He swallows.

The taste is sweet. But not yet sweet enough.

Now, only the manuscript's face remains barren, only the forehead and cheeks, and the sharply pointed little chin. The poet addresses his quill to these empty landscapes next.

"I dream in heat," he whispers. "Of bell-loud nights where I tattoo love in her flesh with the wet needle of my tongue."

Again the scent arises from the manuscript, an odor of arousal and fear, tinged with a patina of copper sweat. The poet lays his quill aside; he removes the satin gag that stills the voice he now craves to hear.

Her whimpers draw him to her mouth. Her chains rattle as he releases the cuffs that bind her at ankles and wrists. With hunger, she strips away his robe; she entwines him with her limbs. The ink of his poems smears between them as it erases beneath a different kind of rhythm, a renga of movement that ends with a syllable of sighs.

Later, as they lie in ink and sex stained sheets, she recalls for him the bargain they had made. Her trust, for his. He nods and she removes her chains and places them upon *his* limbs. She bathes him with her tongue, dries him with her hair. She silences his mouth with satin so he can still taste the wetness of her mouth with his.

Now *she* becomes the poet and he the manuscript. But she composes without ink or sharpened quill. Her marks are inscribed with teeth and nails, written in the red of blood.

WHAT WAS ASKED;
WHAT WAS GIVEN

The dry road was shaded in a hundred crosses, and in the drift of raven wings that spilled the sunlight. It was not yet midday. But the east wind was already white with heat, and its snap was loud as it whipped through dead men's rags and through the right angles of the wood. The peasants hanging on that wood did not mind the wind. For a while they had been warriors and rebels more than peasants, but now they were mostly bones and tatters, with eyeless sockets that stared blankly north along a way called Crucifixion. The dead men did not see the movement in that distance but it was there. A woman came walking in gray. On her face was a need, on her lips a prayer.

The woman's name was Tanquil and she was immensely tired, both from her long, long walk, and from the weight of the pain she carried in her womb. She leaned on a bent stick she'd pulled from a ditch piled high with axe-ravaged trees, and the dust had turned to mud in the sweat of her ankles. The shadows of the crosses did not cool her when she came among them.

At the foot of the seventeenth cross, Tanquil stopped and looked up. The thing on the wood did not resemble anyone she knew, but her thoughts painted it with gray-washed hair and sun-browned flesh. Her hands reached out to touch the feet, and her fingers added the memory of taut skin and calluses. She closed her eyes and could smell his body after they had loved, could feel again the silk of his teeth in her breast.

"Arrin," she murmured to herself. And, "Goddess give me

strength."

Kneeling at the foot of the cross, Tanquil pulled her flaxen skirt away to bare her knees to the earth. From a heavy bag at her right side she took a whip. It was thin-bladed, with a black handle only a hand's-breadth long and nine streamers of bull-hide spreading out like nettles from the base. It was the kind of scourge the Temeri theocracy used on the victims of its crucifixions, especially if they were vampyre. Tanquil hated that term. Vampyre! She much preferred the name her people had chosen when they put aside the night and the hunt—Mutari Kana. "Goddess beloved."

But the hurtfulness of words was not her business here. Another pain was more important. Tanquil gripped the scourge tightly and began to use it against the dust in front of her, ranging back and forth with steady movements that left stripes on the road and bared the pebbles in its bed. One hundred strokes she gave, saving the last two for her knees. The lash cut deeply into her skin and spilled blood that trickled down into the scars she'd made in the road. She nodded her head in satisfaction.

Again Tanquil reached into her bag, and this time she came out with a small copper vial sealed with wax. Before breaking the seal, she looked up at her husband's body on the cross. Her glance was caught by the corpse's left hand, and by the missing little finger that had once worn their binding ring.

Thinking of that finger, Tanquil used the nail of her own finger to break the wax on the vial. Then she upended the tube over the whip marks she'd made in the dirt, and a chalk white powder spilled out in a fine mist to settle over the blood that had poured down from her knees. While that mist settled, Tanquil's hands twisted and twined with a life of their own, as if she held a mortar and pestle and ground bone and dried skin into dust. Tears rolled on her cheeks but she felt only a faint sense of loss. She might no longer have a fetish to remind her of her husband, but she hoped soon to have something to honor him more.

Upon the bed she had made from bone and blood, Tanquil laid out the last items from her sack. There was a pinch of good dirt, a ripening egg, the bulb of a honeyflower, a few stalks of fruiting grain, and the carefully preserved fetus she'd lost from her womb the week before, after the Temeri novitiates had come to tell her the place and manner of her husband's death, after they had thrown Arrin's finger at her feet and stayed on to beat her belly with their lances.

Two centuries ago the Mutari Kana had returned to the soil, taking up again the clothes of mortality and putting away the skins of predators. In a vast sharing of flesh and power they had created their own Goddess. From one of their number they had chosen, and to that one they had given all. And when the one was filled with the glamour of thousands, the rest were empty, were no longer vampyre. Only for the sharing of parent and child, of husband and wife, did they keep the ritual of blood. It became a sacrament of family.

But when the Temeri priesthood rose to power, the name vampyre was resurrected. The word was a constant rain of spit in the faces of Tanquil's people, in the stalls of the markets, in the laws that bound them like mummies. The Goddess had disappeared; some said she'd fled in fear. Others claimed the priests had imprisoned her. Or slain her.

Tanquil had raised her brother and sister after her mother was taken by the priests for breaking a law, and it was not until she was already past the usual age of childbearing that she felt free to bind herself to Arrin. As with all her people, it had taken her a long time to conceive, and she knew she would never do so again. This dead one was the only child she would ever have of her own.

So many dead ones, she thought. Since the theocracy had replaced the population-swamped states of the old world, there had been so many dead, men and women who resisted them, children who cried too loud when their parents were killed, the elders who dared call on a Goddess whose worship was proscribed. Even the animals had gone to fill priestly bellies, and croplands disappeared under the hooves of warhorses. Then Arrin had gone to fight them, and had not come home.

Tanquil looked down at the blanket-bound child she had carried so far, both inside and outside of her body, and she reached out and turned back the cloth from the white-filmed eyes that had petrified at the very moment when they should have been seeing for the first time. *Yes*! There had been so many unanswered deaths that Tanquil could not stand one more. She wanted—she needed—to make some gesture, to bring some bit of life out of all the destruction, no matter how small a life it might be. If she could just grow a flower here, or a stalk of wheat. If her child could be the root of a new vigor, then its death could be tolerated and its mother could live on in hope of better years.

Tanquil was no magic woman, no sorceress, as her ancestors might well have been considered. She knew only how to plant and nurture and pick. But there was one spell she had taught herself through long days in the fields, one tiny skein of words meant for the growing, for the swift building of tissue that would fill the harvest baskets. She didn't know if it had ever worked, if the Goddess had ever heard and lent it strength. But it was the only thing she had to try and change the world. She leaned forward and whispered the words as quietly as she could.

"To the seed give earth, to the stalk water. To the fruit give wing."

Tanquil *believed* in her Goddess. She could not imagine that the Goddess had fled, or died. So now, Tanquil held an image in her head of a woman who was even lonelier than *she* was, and she believed so hard that sweat wicked out of her pores to sheen her face. Power answered her belief.

On all the bodies, on all the crosses, the chests split open to the sky and something came out from those openings, something chatoyant that had waited for just such a moment. A coalescence formed, pearled out of vermilion and pale gray, out of indigo and violet, out of ochre and mahogany black. In another instant, the interplay of light broke apart once more and all its rainbow fingers rippled downward to strike the road in front of Tanquil.

The earth erupted, dust spinning into a vortex that sucked the sweetness out of the air around her. Choking for breath, the woman fell backwards to the ground, her eyes blinking shut to protect them from dirt and swirling pebbles. Her empty womb spasmed once, twice, and again. She shrieked as a bitter pain ripped deep into her abdomen like the stroke of poisoned steel. Then the pain moved out of her body to hover in the world beyond.

For just a moment more, Tanquil refused to open her eyes and see what she had wrought. She had hoped for a token, some bit of life from death. But it seemed clear that more had occurred than she had expected. That suspicion proved true when she finally dredged up the courage to look.

The road where Tanquil had laid out her child and her charms was swept bare, and beneath Arrin's cross a woman was standing—a girl really. She looked no more than fourteen, and though she was unclothed she did not seem naked. The fine hair of her head was colored like the shells of ripened wheat and there was a translucence about her skin, as if Tanquil were staring into the depths of an onion, or through the fragile membrane of a hatching egg. Only when the woman looked into the girl's face did she discover a flaw in what had seemed perfection. There were no pupils amid the bone-white expanse of the eyes.

Tanquil moaned, half in sorrow for the girl, half for herself. Her spell had raised more of a life than she could have hoped for, but that life had already been scarred by pain. Tanquil feared that her emotions were responsible for the pain. She blamed the thread of hatred that had wound its way through her thoughts ever since the day her daughter had been born in blood alone, instead of in blood and water together.

Always, the Goddess had taught against hatred. Anger could be a pure and holy flame sometimes, when it strengthened a tired will to its task. But hatred was a fireplace too full of ashes to burn. Tanquil had tried to sweep out her hate, but it seemed there'd been enough ashes left to sour her casting. Now, instead of creating hope to ease her own suffering, she was left with the work of easing another's. It was what she had always done, though, and she knew she could do it again. This girl-child needed her.

Tanquil struggled to her feet, her muscles aching as if with a day's work in the fields, but her mind was clear and she felt it center on the task at hand. When she straightened her cramped shoulders, she saw that the girl had moved on silent feet and stood just in front of her. The blind eyes were as featureless as pearls. Yet, the older woman sensed a light and a promise behind them, like seeing zephyr moths in the winter and dreaming of spring. For a moment she thought she heard the whisper of words: *The flower is born.*

Tanquil wiped her face and held out her hand. "Come, daughter," she said. "We've a long way to go and much to speak of on the way."

The girl lifted her own hand until their wrists met and their fingers interlaced. She smiled radiantly and Tanquil smiled back, though she knew the other couldn't see it. Then the woman linked arms with the girl and they started walking west away from the road. It was the way of the Goddess, the way of forgiveness and hope. There was nowhere else for them to go.

* * * * * * *

Tanquil did not glance back at the crucifixes where they cast the shadows of their burdens across the land. Only the girl looked, and wherever her blind gaze touched the corrupted earth, stalks of wild grain burst forth and bloomed with white flowers. The plants continued to grow long after the Goddess looked away, and after a while they entwined the crosses and their blossoms turned to red, lending to the wood and the dead a kind of glory.

FLAGELLATED

Mouths of Sorrow: Tasting of Pearl
Ivory Coin: Lyre Winds
Voices are Torn: White with Fear
Drum and Kiss: Whip of Wind

blood
sutures: tongues
bones

Lace and Silk: Wet with Love
Caress to Sweat: Spent and Empty
Black Lips: Whore Eyes
Fail to Oblivion: Sweet rotted Red

SACRIFICIAL

LOUD LOVE

She wears her love loud in her face,
in the wanton weave of her fingers
in my hair.
She plays her song of wicked bells
and my soul shivers to the sound
as I kneel.
Her hands press, drawing me to her,
bringing me to the lovely oblivion
between her thighs.
She murmurs a soft litany of want,
as she bids me satisfy my hunger,
and hers.

WHEN THE WHITE MIST

He comes out of the forest with fog wreathing his slender frame. And embers sing in his eyes while his mouth drips shadows.

The pale woman with silken hair looks up from the rock where she sits sketching the bright, full moon. She glimpses the man, but does not recognize him for what he is until his dark-feathered wings spread and he closes the gap between them in an instant.

She leaps up, half finished drawing fluttering away as she tries to run. But hands upon which the nails are long and white catch her shoulders and spin her to the ground. Pinned under his weight, she catches breath to scream, until his body softens over hers and his wings enfold her like warm ashes.

She wonders if he is angel or demon. Then it doesn't matter as he lowers his mouth to hers. In that kiss is the innocence of a child and the stench of heaven burning. On his lips she tastes blood and ruins. She tastes candle smoke and spider web dust, morning dew and waterfalls.

And when his tongue seeks to enter, she makes room, not knowing whether he feeds her or steals from her, not caring. She wants the erotic oblivion he offers.

Long after, she awakens with her body bruised and her hair tangled with dirt and leaves. She wears his scent on her skin, clinging like silk.

Rising weakly, she makes her way home, forgetting her sketch pad and charcoals. And she never questions why, for long years after, she shivers in the fog. Or why she likes to walk at night...

When the white mist comes.

MOTH

Warm Soul
Dark
Daggered heart
Beating
Wings
And I see her with the blood from razors
Scraped with the bane fires of Hell
I see her mouth strung to white
Her love turned
to dust
to void
Until she rises
Cloaked with sin
Vast in desire to hate

SOFT

She likes my soul all soft,
begging for touch,
the arc of love between us
shocking my lips

She likes the sweet skin
beneath my sweat,
the taste of sun lingering
inside my mouth

She likes to know things
she cannot know,
through the life she draws
from my throat.

THORN

Hugh opened his eyes on darkness, awakened by a trickle of cool air that found his spine and slid along it. He rolled over to find the bed empty beside him, the covers pushed back so the breeze from the AC could slip under. A glance at the luminous dial of his watch on the bedside table told him it was just after midnight, but he could already feel the beginnings of the hangover he would have in the morning. His mouth and eyes felt dry and a hollow buzzing filled his head. He cursed, then threw back the sheets and came to his feet, only to wince as the wooden floor sent cold running in shivers up his legs. Quickly slipping on house shoes and tossing on an old robe, Hugh went down the stairs, through the empty kitchen, and out into the backyard, knowing where he'd find his wife. Sarah would be with her flowers, her precious flowers.

As expected, she was there, her pale hair shining in the moonlight. She knelt among freshly turned earth near the far end of the yard, digging a hole for the rosebush that lay wrapped in damp newspaper beside her. Hugh strode toward her, the tall grass slapping wetly at his ankles. She looked up at his approach and brushed a stray feather of hair back from her cheek.

"How many more of these damn things do you need?" he asked her, gesturing at the bush. "The yard is full of them already."

And he was right. Everywhere, the flowers reached toward the sky. In the moonlight, all the blooms looked either white or black, but Hugh knew there were at least a dozen colors and shades among them, yellow, pink, red, and white, as well as purple ones so dark they were almost black.

Sarah had told him once in one of her melodramatic moods that the yard looked like the place where rainbows fell when they were broken. He'd laughed at her then but he wasn't laughing now. Roses had become her obsession. She spent every minute she could in this yard, fertilizing, watering, pollinating, and even talking to a bunch of bushes. And now she was out here in the middle of the night planting another one.

"I'm sorry," Sarah said. "I didn't mean to wake you."

"But you did. At least you could pull the sheets back up when you get out of bed. I woke up with my ass freezing off. You always keep the AC so damn cold."

"I'm sorry," she said again, her eyes falling to the garden spade in her hands so she could avoid his gaze.

"For God's sake, woman," he said, exasperated by the hang-dog look she put on every time he got angry with her. "Show a little spunk sometime. You act like a pup that's been beat."

She bit her lip and looked back up at him.

He sighed and shook his head. "Come back to bed. You spend too much time in this garden."

"All right. It'll just take a second to plant this one bush."

"Do it tomorrow."

"But—"

"I said do it tomorrow!" Hugh shouted. Then he grabbed up the plant, ignoring the thorns that stabbed into his hand, and threw it over the fence into the empty lot behind their place. "Better yet, don't plant it! You've got enough."

"Hugh," Sarah protested.

He took her arm and half helped her, half dragged her to her feet. "You leave that thing out there. I don't wanna come home tomorrow and find you've picked it up. You hear me?"

He glared at her until she nodded.

"Now come to bed," he said.

She turned toward the house dutifully enough and he followed her, wondering what on earth had possessed him to marry her.

She had the sense of a cow and all the backbone of a rutabaga.

He hesitated for a moment at the kitchen door, feeling a tiny wind reach up under his robe and touch his back coldly. He turned and heard it sighing among the flowers as if in sadness, or anger. Then he shook his head. He rubbed the bristles on his face, thinking that his wife's silliness was starting to affect him. He shook his head again and followed her up the stairs.

They lay down together, and when Sarah turned away Hugh reached for her. He ignored her meek protests and slid the nightgown off her shoulders. He fell asleep soon afterward to the sound of her silence.

Toward morning, Hugh dreamed. He seldom remembered his dreams but this one he'd not forget. It was the third night in a row his mind had played it for him. He was standing in the yard and it was very cold. The wind was blowing. Or at least the roses seemed to feel it, though he could not. Then he noticed that each flower moved as if to its own small mistral, and he shivered with more than cold. He took a step closer to the blooms, drawn though he did not wish it, and something struck his ankle from behind. He leaped, in slow motion, spinning, and came around expecting to see a snake coiled at his feet. Instead, he saw only vines that reared like snakes and two thorns with rosary beads of blood at their tips.

Hugh woke suddenly, sweaty from the dream. Then something scratched at the window and he wasn't sure whether the dream was finished or not. He sat up, heart pounding, a yell starting in his throat, but before it surfaced he saw the shadows against the glass and knew it was only the roses Sarah had trained to run up a trellis at the side of the house. They had grown fast and half covered the window to the bedroom. The wind blew the thorns against the pane and it must have been that which triggered his dream, and those of the last two nights as well.

Forcing the dreams out of his mind, Hugh stumbled down to the dining room where he found Sarah hunched over a cup of hot coffee and one of her ubiquitous flower magazines.

Jeez! Wouldn't the woman ever get enough?

"You think you could put that down long enough to fix me some breakfast?" he asked.

She got up quickly and went into the kitchen, only to return a moment later with a napkin covered tray. Beneath the napkin were eggs, bacon, and another cup of coffee. There were also two aspirin. That made him angry, even though he needed them. He would almost rather she yelled than be so damn solicitous of him. But hell, he'd only had a few drinks anyway. It wasn't like he'd stayed out late or anything. He'd been home by ten. But Sarah—good old Sarah—had been right there waiting for him, the loving wife. He knew she just did it to make him feel guilty. Well, he was not about to let her win on that one.

"Stupid woman," he muttered under his breath.

"I already had your breakfast ready," Sarah said.

Hugh only grunted. "And the paper?"

She went to get it and then sat down across from him while he ate and read the morning news. She fetched his lunch when he was finished and stood waiting for her goodbye kiss. He pecked her cheek.

"I won't be late," he said.

He tossed the paper down beside the empty breakfast dishes and nodded toward them. "I hope you plan to do something besides play in the garden all day. This house could use a little work."

"I'll clean it," she said.

"Good," he said, as he bussed her cheek again and went out.

He was five minutes late for work and, of course, the boss was waiting at his office when he got there. He glanced at the clock as Hugh came in but said nothing about the time. Instead, he tossed a sheaf of papers on Hugh's already cluttered desk.

"The ad you cooked up for the Dorsey account needs work," he said.

"What's wrong with it?" Hugh asked.

"Hell, look at it! If you can't figure it out you shouldn't be working here."

Hugh said nothing as the man walked away. Inside he was raging. "One of these days," he muttered. "One of these days I'm going to kick that son-of-a-bitch's ass."

Things had started badly and they only got worse throughout the day. Inanimate objects attacked him all morning and he kept wondering what was in it for them. He put a staple through his finger; the flap of an envelope cut his lip. His paper clips and pens had gone AWOL, and to make matters still worse the girl in the next cubical had a new boyfriend who'd sent her roses. As if Hugh didn't get enough of them at home.

The flowery smell grew stronger and stronger until Hugh thought he'd gag on it. Once, he got up to demand that the woman get rid of the things, but when he passed her desk the boss was talking to her. The blooms were all opened toward him, he noted, as if watching him go by. They were bright red, like his blood in last night's dream. He decided on an early lunch.

At a local bar and grill, Hugh ran into his first spot of luck in weeks, a businessman willing to listen to some talk about advertising. Turned out the fellow was in the market for the right ad and Hugh quickly invited him home for dinner. He had several more drinks after the man left and almost forgot to phone Sarah. He finally called her about 4:00 and felt himself getting angrier and angrier as the phone buzzed without an answer. She picked up on the eighth ring and for a moment Hugh said nothing.

"Hugh, is that you?" she finally asked.

"You were in the yard again weren't you?"

"Well, I was just—"

"I know what the hell you were *just* doing. Working with your precious *flowers*. Well, I'm telling you right now. You start doing your other work or I'm going to take an axe to your roses."

"Hugh, no!"

"Hugh, no," he mimicked. "Yes, Sarah, yes. I'll turn them all into confetti."

It was Sarah's turn to be silent.

Hugh took a deep breath to get hold of himself, then said in a calmer voice: "I called to tell you a potential client is coming over for dinner. He'll be there about 7:00 so you better get started fixing something decent. And stay out of the yard!"

He punched the button to end the call before she could reply.

Hugh was surprised to find Sarah in the kitchen when he got home about 6:00. He fixed himself a drink and carried it over to where she was working. She had just opened the oven and the rich, dark smell of roast wafted up to his nose.

"Now that's more like it," he said. She lip-smiled in return, though her eyes didn't follow.

The potential client arrived a little after 7:00 and Hugh immediately fixed him a drink, along with another for himself. He was starting to feel the effects of the liquor but told himself it only loosened him up and made him a better salesman. The client made the usual inane comments about how lovely the house was, then happened to glance out the picture window at the back where his eyes caught on Sarah's roses.

"Beautiful," he said, and this time Hugh could tell he meant it. Sarah, who had just come out of the kitchen, beamed as if it were her children the man was complimenting.

"Would you like to see them?" she asked, and the man accepted before Hugh could protest. He had no choice but to follow them out into the yard, though that was the last place he wanted to be. He was deathly sick of roses. He noted that the grass was wet and silver beads of water glistened on the flower petals. It hadn't rained today so Sarah had been in the yard even after he warned her against it.

Well, he thought to himself, *I'll do something about that later.*

The client rhapsodized on and on about flowers, asking Sarah a thousand questions about hers, about their care, their fertilizer, their watering schedule. *Will he never stop?* Hugh wondered. *Next he'll be asking how often the roses get laid.*

Surreptitiously, Hugh kicked a bush and felt a smug satisfaction as several buds fell off onto the wet earth. He almost smiled and at the same moment glanced up to catch Sarah's eyes on him, as if she knew what he had done. There was something in the paleness of her face that he'd never seen before. Almost, it could have been hatred. But he knew it would not be *that* emotion from dear old Sarah, though he felt the stiffness of her arm as he took it. He forced a smile for the client's sake and reached out to stroke a bloom. An instant later he was jerking back, staring in surprise at the bead of blood on his thumb.

"The damn thing bit me," he said.

The client chuckled. "Some people always seem to find the thorns," he said.

Hugh chuckled with him, though he did not find it terribly funny.

The night, like the day, went from bad to worse. Dinner was excellent but Hugh scarcely tasted it. He knew he was drinking too much but could not seem to stop. Sarah and the client spent the entire time talking about flowers and when the fellow left there'd been almost no discussion of business. So much for having something to appease the boss with tomorrow.

It's all Sarah's fault, Hugh thought. *Hers and her roses.*

He poured himself a whiskey straight and plopped down in front of the television. Sarah tried to get him to come up to bed but he ignored her, refusing to even say goodnight. At last, she went upstairs alone. Hugh remained in the living room, now and then glancing up from the images on the TV to see the darkness-filled hollow of the backyard. The night hid the flowers and he was glad of that. But he still knew they were there.

After a while, Hugh fell asleep in his chair from a combination of alcohol and mental exhaustion, and the *dream* returned to him. This time it was worse. The thorns struck at him again and again, rearing up high on his body. And he could not move. The wind howled. The thorns tore at his legs, chewed at his arms, flashed toward his eyes. He woke with a yell. The TV was full of static, as if the cable had gone out, but over the white noise he heard another sound, a stealthy scratching, scratching at the walls and windows. The rose bushes were moving against the house, dragging thorns over dry wood and cool glass.

I have to get rid of them, he thought. *Else I'll never have another peaceful night's sleep. I've got to get rid of them. I've got to get rid of them. Rid of them, rid of them.*

The thoughts were as loud inside his head as the thorns were outside. Driven almost by a compulsion, Hugh got up and staggered toward the door and out into the yard. Near the back fence stood the little metal shed where Sarah kept her gardening tools. In it, Hugh found a hoe and shears. He dragged the tools out and carried them toward the trellises at the back of the house.

"I'll start there," he muttered. "Where the worst of them are."

* * * * * * *

Sarah opened her eyes on the morning. She rolled over to find the bed empty beside her. Hugh's side had not been slept in. She stretched and half smiled, happy to be alone for a moment. She'd have to get up soon to fix Hugh's breakfast but she could lay here another minute or two.

Thoughts of Hugh destroyed her smile. He'd been drinking and that would leave him in a foul mood all day. She wondered sometimes if she still loved her husband, or if she were only going through the motions of marriage out of habit. He'd often been cold to her in the last few years, but he'd not *always* been that way. There had been good times but the drinking seemed to have changed him. She sighed and got up to check on him.

Sarah was surprised when she failed to find her husband in the living room where she'd left him. Nor was he in the kitchen. The yard was the last place she thought to look but that was where she found him. He was standing near the house, leaning against a trellis of roses as if asleep. She started forward, and froze as she saw the vines looped around his waist and the thorns buried through his clothes and into his pale hands. She looked up to where the roses bloomed over his chalky face. They were more crimson than she had ever seen them, especially since they had been white the day before.

THE LADY WORE BLACK

The lady wore black, with green in her eyes, and there was the frost of years in her hair though it had not yet touched her face. I watched her often as she came down to the shore of an evening, as I sat unnoticed on a pier out over the ocean where I could paint the waves called by ancient ritual to break themselves on the sand. The lady was like the waves, and I watched her and wondered.

Once each month, always on the same day and at the same time, the woman came to this spot. She would stand at the edge of the surf, whether it rained or did not, and she would bow her head for a moment as if in prayer. Then she would raise flashing white hands and throw something dark into the sea to be drawn out by the currents. One day I brought binoculars with me, and I saw that it was roses she gave to the water, roses so dark as to be black.

Four times I watched and sketched the lady before she turned one evening and looked down the long beach toward me, her attention caught, perhaps, by a glint of dying sunlight off the lenses of my glasses. After that, she turned to look for me whenever she came.

And one evening she waved.

Later that night I collected my sketches and locked myself in my room to paint her. It took all the dark hours, but at dawn I knew I had captured her. I painted her silhouette against a sky and sea that were lighter than they should have been, but just the color they seemed when she was there. I painted her in black, with night stroked hair and a porcelain face, and I made her eyes green, though not at the time having seen their true color. Afterward, I sat through the day with a bottle of wine for company, nourishing myself from her portrait and falling in love. At twilight I drew black flowers in her arms.

I could not help but have questions concerning the lady. Who was she? Why did she give roses to the sea? I wanted to know, most of all, why she always turned and looked for me when her ritual was done. Sometimes, the answer to that last question seemed so important that I drew the responses I wanted into her portrait, or into the few smaller paintings I did of her. Sometimes the question itself seemed only a dream, and it was never easy to wait until the next month, until the next time I would see her.

Obsession is such a phony word and is used for so many phony things, but I know of no other term to explain my attraction for the woman. Her image interfered with my work until even an act as simple as cleaning brushes became an unpleasant chore. It distracted me from thoughts of her. I invented a hundred things to say in introducing myself, and discarded them all again for fear that an awkward gesture or odd turn of phrase might send her away. Too, I was a little afraid of what she might say to me, of what she might do to destroy the portrait I held of her. It was only when my dreams started to end in tears that I knew something had to change, and I waited at the shore on the day of her next visit.

She was late that evening. Because of my presence, I was sure. Still, I did not leave, and at last she came, walking out on the sand from across a headland of rock that jutted from the western end of the beach into the cold ocean waters. I stood without moving and the lady came up near without speaking. Her dress was of midnight silk, an ebon wedding gown, but there were red sandals on her feet.

She walked down until the water came up and splashed against the hem of the dress, and she stood for a moment before throwing her flowers in. We studied them together until they were only a darker splotch against the shadow-darkened sea, and then she turned her eyes to me. They danced with light and were a deep river-green, just as I had painted them.

She looked at me and I wanted to speak. I needed to speak. But my tongue would not work, and after a bit she turned away. The fear of seeing her walk off with mysteries blocked up in her throat galvanized me to action and I held her with a word.

"Stay."

She hesitated, looking into me and through me. I do not believe she wished to go, and I realized she must have been very lonely. This, too, was the way I had painted her.

"Tell me your name," I said at last.

"It is Rachel."

"Mine is Robert."

"A nice name," she said.

"So is Rachel," I said. "A dark name to fit a dark lady."

"Not so dark," she said, looking out to where the flowers had disappeared into the distance. "Not so dark as roses or the sea."

"I do not understand," I said, and knew instantly that it was a mistake. A brief emptiness crossed her face and she made a move to go.

"Wait," I said, afraid I'd lost her. "It's really none of my concern, I know. It's just that I was wondering. I—" Then I stopped as she turned back toward me.

"I'm sorry," I said again.

She spoke then, her voice flat, without music. "The roses are for my husband," she told me. "He died at sea, but the flowers will call him home. He died at sea ten years ago, but the flowers..." Her words withered away.

"For ten years you've been coming to this place," I said. I did not intend a question but she responded as if I had.

"Ten years almost to the day," she said. "I've counted the hours and the months, numbered the years, and yes, I know my husband is not coming home. But I thought. I hoped...."

"For something," I said.

"For something," she agreed.

I reached a hand and her shoulders slumped. I put my arms around her and she began to cry, the tears running down the front of my shirt. For ten years she must have bottled those tears up, for they ran from her eyes a long time. Only gradually did her shudders fade, and when they were over I lifted her sorrow-heated face up to mine and kissed her on the lips. She did not resist, and after a moment returned the kiss, as if that too she had held back for ten years. That night I followed her around the headland to her house, and I loved her as softly as I could. Neither of us cared about the mistakes in the other.

By the end of the week I'd moved in with Rachel. No words were ever spoken concerning it. One day I was just there and did not go home again. The transition was easy. I had little in the way of belongings anyway, a few clothes, my palettes and brushes, my pictures of her. She cried out when she saw those likenesses, and after that I would occasionally find her standing and looking at them, as if surprised that another could see her as beautiful. The paintings left no doubt as to how I saw her.

Our time together in that place was pleasant. During the days we walked the shore, picking up shells and throwing stones, listening to the gulls scream and the waves beat on the sand. In the evening I painted, turning out more work in hours than in weeks before. Most of it had Rachel's form hidden somewhere in the canvas.

Even money was not a real concern. I had some from my paintings, and from my past, and Rachel did well selling local plants and flowers out of the small hothouse in her yard. It came as no surprise to find that one strain of her roses grew almost black, though she never sold any of those. No, we did not have a lot of cash, but Rachel's house was paid for and we made enough to live by.

On weekends we loaded up her old Volkswagen with paintings and flowers and drove the distance into New Orleans to sell them in Jackson Square. Rachel's appearance helped and a good Saturday usually netted us enough to make it through the rest of the week, and sometimes even enough to let us stay late in town for a movie in some out of the way theater. Mostly, though, we hurried home to the sea and the quiet of the night. Sometimes, while Rachel slept, I would feel the need and take up my brushes and paint again. My best work was done in those hours, and when I fed my body off those images it was like a sacrament on my tongue, like a sanctification of the unholy. It kept me alive.

It was not long before I had a month's worth of canvases. I thought little of it until I found Rachel among her flowers one afternoon, dressed in black and picking dark roses. Then I realized how many days had passed. I watched her for a time, saying nothing, but when she stood to go I drew her to me and would not release her. I pulled her into the house and to the bed, and she cried again that night, though less than before. I rocked her in my arms until she slept, and soon fell off into slumber myself.

Rachel was not with me when I awoke. It was still early and I feared she had returned to the sea after all. But she had not gone far. I found her in the hothouse, kneeling among her flowers to cut down the black roses. I hoped this marked the beginning of forgetting, but was afraid that it only meant resignation. I went and put my hands on her shoulders, and she smiled up at me as she clipped the last stem and let the flower fall. She stood and I took her hand, squeezing it tightly as we left the plant nursery. At the steps of her cottage we stopped to watch the surf pound the beach.

"It was foolish of me wasn't it?" she asked after a while.

"What?" I returned, though I was sure I knew.

"The flowers," she said. "I thought that if I didn't forget him, then somehow, somewhere, he would know and would come home. We were both so alone before we married, and I grew to love him very much."

"I know you did," I said. "And the flowers weren't foolish. Somewhere he did see, and he knows how you feel."

"I hope," she said.

Then she turned her face up to be kissed. "But I love you too," she added.

I liked to hear her words, though I knew by the way she spoke that she did not really mean them. She would put away thoughts of her husband for me, but they would never be gone and I would never have the whole Rachel to love. I could not bear to have her stand half-empty beside me. I loved her enough to care more for *her* happiness than for my own, loved her enough to take all the power inside of me at that moment and hurl it at the sea.

It was never pigment and oil that I needed to paint. The canvas always lived in my head. And I painted now, with only the filaments of my mind, the absolutely best image I could. It was fashioned out of cold darkness and wasted time, and from it I drank and drank until the sweetness filled my veins and pulsed outward as invisible white streamers. Then I poured it all back into the mold I had made, and I said a prayer that had not touched my lips in a very long age. The whole thing was done in an instant, and I collapsed on the doorstep of Rachel's house when it was finished.

She was beside me on her knees when I opened my eyes again. Into her worried face, I smiled and said I was fine. She helped me to my feet and we stood there, with me looking beyond her toward the ocean. A dog howled, far off, its voice echoing across the water, and behind the dog's voice came another sound, like the foaming of a ship's prow through waves. Too, there was the distant clanging of a ship's bell. Suddenly, Rachel grew stiff in my arms.

We stood and waited, she not knowing why, our ears straining against the constant boom of the surf. But it was our eyes that told us of a visitor coming. I saw his shape in the moonlight as he rounded the headland to the east and started up toward Rachel's cottage, plodding along with his gaze turned down, dragging one leg behind him for slow step after slow step, moving as if filled with immense tiredness. Rachel gasped beside me and I did not ask her why.

Stone stairs led down to the beach from the grassy shelf where Rachel's cottage sat. The visitor came up them slowly, laboriously—though I could not hear that his breathing was harsh—and walked through the rusted iron gate into the yard where we stood. I knew who he was and did not need to see him any closer. But he moved forward anyway, stepping into the light that fell through one window of the house.

In that light our guest's face was shockingly pale, like sculptor's clay, and there was a saltwater sheen spread over his features like a second layer of skin. I stared as his throat began to writhe. He was trying to speak, I thought, until I saw the stem of a rose slip out between his teeth and fall to earth. Then he was leaning forward, shudders racking his frame as the petals and stems and thorns of a thousand roses began to spill from his body onto the stone flaggings of Rachel's yard. All were colored black, just like the sightless staring of his eyes.

Rachel stepped forward to embrace him when he finished, and there was the phosphor gleam of an exchanged kiss, the dark movement of the dead man's limbs as he entwined them about his wife. I could see now why she had chosen this man. He was as handsome as she was beautiful. I studied them together for a moment, then took from my pocket one of the roses that Rachel had so recently cut and carried it forward as an offering. I knelt as I handed it to him, and he plucked one of the dark petals and laid it upon my tongue like a host. I held it in my mouth for a moment, as a whirlwind of flowers lifted up and danced around us, and I swallowed just as Rachel stroked my hair with a sea-dampened hand.

The bitterness of the petal was still on my tongue when Rachel and her husband lay down on a quilt of silk-soft roses. They beckoned for me to join them, and it was like coming home for me too. Later, I would paint the three of us together, a lovely, humpbacked woman, a drowned cripple, a lonely vampire who only wanted to love them both and who had the power to love them forever.

Rachel didn't notice until later that I had brought the dead flowers back to life too. In both flowers and in man I had fashioned well, as I would do for her in the year of her death.

FRAGMENTS

He studied her from inches away, his gaze drifting the length of her body as she lay pale against the black leather sheets.

"Did you dream?" he asked, topping her, entering her, tangling his limbs with hers.

"I dreamt in sweat," she replied, her breath catching, her body growing languid beneath his. "Of cinnamon skins and wet mouths and kisses."

"I dreamt too," he said. His hands slid into the wild tousle of her hair. His hips rocked against hers. "I dreamt that I was more than just your imagination."

She smiled, and closed the book on her lover.

COLD BLOOD

Her teeth lay against my throat, sharp, caressing, full of want.

"It is cold, I said.

She spoke not.

"Very cold," I said.

She said nothing, but I felt her teeth move and the veins opened to bleed.

"I love you," I said. "Did you hear? I *love* you."

"It is cold," she replied.

MAPS

Punctures left by her teeth
leak life onto the floor,
staining the cracks,
the impurities in the wood.
She touches those marks as I die,
her finger tracing lines,
drawing maps in red,
her tongue erasing them.

RORSCHACH GOD

The wind uses the forest to voice its thoughts. It uses the pinions of owls. I hear the words, though I do not know the language. The dragonflies understand. The geckos do, with their flanks working like bellows in the sun.

Sitting on my deck, I listen to the clack of wooden wind chimes, the tink-tink of copper ones. Something caws in the distance. I think it is a crow. Or something mimicking a crow. My ears keep me grounded. But my eyes are lost in greenery.

Not twenty yards from where my chair sits on my deck, the woods rise. Pines. Oaks. Magnolias. Other trees I cannot name. Spanish moss twists along their limbs like the beards of old men. Blackberry brambles fill the underbrush, gravid with yet unripened fruit. Things are hiding among the green, though with a little effort I can see them.

Shadows sweep across the world with wings. Perhaps there are birds high in the air casting them. My human mind tells me there are birds. But I do not see them; I cannot swear they exist. And the shadows are large. I think perhaps they are fossil shadows, leftovers from the time of pteranodons and pterodactyls.

But the living things that fill the woods are not fossils. A moment ago a long silken blackness raced down the bare trunk of a pine. I saw it clearly, an animal shape some three feet long with a sleek head and whippet tail. It took a while for my human mind to say anything about *that*. It told me I'd seen the shadow of one pine swaying past another in the wind. But I recognize lies when I hear them and I don't believe it.

I don't believe it because of the god who conceals himself just below that spot in the bushes. He is painted many shades of green and black, and blends so well with his surroundings that I cannot tell where the god ends and the world begins. Sometimes I see only his eyes, which are like specks of ice reflected in tear drops. Sometimes I see his torn cloak and the ratty top hat he wears. I have never seen his mouth. I don't know if he smiles. I wonder if he has teeth, and if they are long.

The god is watching me, very very quietly watching me. I suspect the silk-black animal is really one of his angels. I'm sure there are more. They are hiding from me, even as the god is *trying* to hide. I believe he has planted the forest on his back in an attempt at camouflage. But the wind reveals him. The voices in the breeze are prayers coming in from worshippers all over the world.

I wonder if the god would join me on the deck if I invited him for a drink and a smoke. I am divided on the subject. The human part of me suggests that he will not leave the woods, that without the glory of his surroundings he would appear only shabby and small. He could not tolerate that. The animal part of me, though, says he's already here, hunched over and dripping behind me.

I wonder if I should turn my head. I wonder if I should show him my own teeth. I don't want to scare him off. I'm very hungry, and it has been a long time since I've eaten a meal as fine as a god.

RIVER ROAD,
NIGHT MUSIC

On a night road she leaped toward him
in his headlights stilled
like the bright edge of a shadow
like a black hole photographed.
She knew so much about gravity
begging death under his wheels
and the wet sound was sharply loud
of circuits breaking in her bones.
When he hit her, hit her, hit her
When he hit her

He pulled off River Road on the levee side and parked on
the shoulder between two telephone poles, one of which bore
ragged gouges in its treated wood. It was 7:56 in the evening.
Late April. Almost dark. With the windows down he could hear
the sound of tugboats pushing barges on the Mississippi River
just beyond the batture. He could *smell* the river, the odor thick-
ened with closer scents of grass, automobile exhaust, fresh cut
orchids.

As if it would protect him from the ruins in his memory, he
sat there quietly in his truck for a moment. Then he took a long,
slow swallow of air and scooped up all but one spray of wild
orchids from the passenger seat. He forced himself to get out
and stand beside the curvy road.

A lone car passed. He waited, then walked out and placed

the bouquet in the center of the right lane. He knew precisely where to put it, though there was no marker and this was the first time he'd been back here since the...accident. Tonight, he'd had to come.

The flowers would soon get run over, bruised into the concrete or scattered and wasted along the highway. He didn't care. It even gave him a grim sense of self-flagellating pleasure to think on beauty being trashed. After all, he considered bitterly, he should be an expert on that subject.

It had rained earlier and a thrum of tires on wet pavement warned him of a car approaching around the curve. Instinct pushed him off the road, to the opposite side from the levee, where he stopped next to a short, rectangular column of red brick that anchored one end of a black, wrought-iron fence. His fingernails stabbed at his palm. It must be almost exactly the same place where she had been standing when he'd come around that curve a few months earlier.

Muscles in his jaws bunched. His teeth ground together as if he were chewing at the hurt in his memory.

The car passed, just missing the flowers, and the splash of its lights made him realize how much darker it had gotten in the last few minutes. Night had slipped up on him unnoticed.

He hated the night. Now.

At his back came wind-stirred whispers and the drip of water. He turned. He stood at the border of a kingdom of oaks. There were maybe twenty huge live oaks here in this lot, most of them thickly bearded with Spanish moss. They were vast and old and he thought he recalled someone saying there had been a plantation here once, and that the house had burned away.

The trees remained, surrounded on three sides by warehouses or small business offices. They provided the only *big* live oaks left along this stretch of River Road, which curved alongside the Mississippi a few miles west of the so called "crescent bend" in which the city of New Orleans nestled. He wondered how many of the trees would survive the real estate development "coming soon" to this area.

Another car went by. He watched it over his shoulder as it tumbled the orchids along the wet black highway. When he turned back to the oaks he saw a woman. Dark sweep of hair. Pale curve of face. A mouth the color of bruised strawberries.

His heart slammed. For a moment he thought it was *the* woman, the one who had darted in front of his pickup on New Year's Eve. The one he'd brought the flowers for. But that couldn't be. No matter how much he might wish it.

A neglected cement drive called Bourgeois Court turned off River Road among the trees and the woman stood in the center of it, beneath the golden haze shed by a pole light. His heart began to steady. Just someone out for an evening stroll, he was sure. Nothing more than coincidence could have brought a woman here at this moment.

Yet, she stood so still. And her hair? Her ivory face? He took a step toward her, something more than curiosity dragging him. The light dimmed. A dust devil whirled up, though the ground was wet. Motes danced in the close air. He blinked.

He saw:

...the railing of a fishing cabin on creosoted pilings over Lake Pontchartrain. A woman draped across it. Her back arched.

He is behind her.

Afternoon rain dimples the lake surface, spreads a moiré mist in beads on their skin. But nothing distracts them from move-ment as he thrusts within her, hips pumping. Her sex tightens around his, milking him.

He gasps a litany of pleasure. Her body jolts. His left hand tightens in the long, tangled promise of her hair. His other hand reaches around her waist, dips between her thighs, fingers finding and shivering against her clitoris. Their hips rock together with liquid sounds, faster and faster. His breath comes panting.

The woman throws her head up and back against his hand, shoves her lower half into his rhythm. Every hair and cell in his body screams alive with the arc and flow of current. He leans over her, teeth finding her shoulder, nipping at the muscle there. He smells the chicory bite of her sweat. Tastes it.

She writhes, straining beneath him, her bare skin slick, her moans rising as her nipples brush back and forth over the use-polished wood of the railing. She slides one hand behind her, her fingers finding his hip, nails digging, jerking, as if to pull him deeper into her heat.

"Please," she says, "please." Wanting. Needing. Begging. Her release. And his....

He cried out, staggered, nearly falling as his release did come—in a jetting spray inside his jeans that left his mouth twisted open in shamed amazement. With pupils shot wide he glanced up, suddenly, horrifyingly embarrassed, sure that the woman among the oaks had witnessed his body's bizarre betrayal.

She was gone.

His head jerked left and right, eyes darting as he looked for her. The pole lights were bright again. If they'd ever been dim. Only at the lot's edges did enough shadows cling to cloak someone. Unless she stood behind a tree. He blushed afresh, thinking that she might be hiding in fear of him after what she'd seen.

He started to turn, to rush away, and glimpsed a dark clot of something lying on the pale cement of the drive where the woman had stood. He hesitated, scanning the lot one more time. There was no sight of her, no sound of her. With a frown, he walked forward, went to one knee beside the...something. He touched softness, picked up a long, thick coil of sable hair as fine and silken as flour.

With fingers clenching in the hair, he remembered—when the woman had leaped in front of his truck and he'd hit her. He remembered running to her, pulling her off the road before another car could come around the curve and hit her again. He remembered slick blood and how part of her scalp had come off in his hands. Her hair had been raven-tinted, shoulder blade length, vividly soft. Just like *this* hair.

He couldn't help himself. He lifted his hand to press the coil of hair to his nose and mouth. Smells of dampness and pollen rasped at his nostrils. But there were other scents—azalea, honeysuckle...orchids. At the moment he'd run her down, the woman had been wearing an orchid behind her ear.

Slow, welling tears found him then. He'd been drinking that *other* night. Two beers. Not enough to be legally drunk. And it had been clear to everyone that the woman had wanted suicide. But he remembered the beers, the driving just a little too fast, remembered glancing down to turn up the radio on *Stairway to Heaven*. He'd wanted it loud and it had been loud when he'd hit her, when an instant later he'd slammed sideways into a telephone pole that still bore the marks.

Metal tinkled, like charm bracelets dancing on slender, weaving wrists.

The sound brought his head up, a quiet sob catching and holding in his throat. Midges roiled about his face in the glow of the pole light. He brushed them from his swollen eyes, let them drink in the salted wetness on his cheeks.

Thoughts of copper charms and symbols filled the space behind his forehead. He recalled them scattered on the shadowed highway like metallic snowflakes—ankhs, scarabs, crosses, Celtic knots, astrological signs of Aries, Taurus, Libra, Pisces. The woman had been wearing them when she'd offered herself to his wheels.

The long climb up from one knee to his feet felt hard; the shiny coil of hair dangled from his hand, wet now with tears. It seemed to him that the tinkling sound had come from the far end of the lot, and his tennis shoes scraped on the cement drive as he moved them along in that direction.

At a fence of unpainted planks marking the back of the property, he halted. Frog voices cracked the gloom. Something tiny whined in his ear. *Mosquito?* There was enough light to outline the weeds and incarnate the massive oak to the left of the drive, which stabbed two wind-twisted limbs to the earth like huge alien fingers. Beyond the bent limbs stood a flat wheel of bricks about two feet high that might once have marked the base of a gazebo. He could see only the edge of it.

The tinkling came again, like coolness in the midst of heat. He stepped around the tree to see a woman standing in the center of the brick wheel. The shadowy lines of lattice walls seemed to imprison her. It must have been a trick of the same light that painted amber streaks in hair that he knew had to be full black.

He stopped very still. A tingling burned in his hand and he felt the sheaf of hair that he held slowly dissolve between his fingers—like cotton candy melting. He glanced down, trying to convince himself that he'd dropped the hair. But logic wasn't working for him just then; the pounding in his chest had hammered it away.

He looked back at the woman. She wore nothing more than a sheet that left bare her shoulders. Her face was turned to one side, her profile full of sharp angles and hollows, softened only by the dark fall of her hair. The breeze licked her makeshift garment against her, rattled the charms on the half dozen copper bracelets that dangled on her right arm.

"Who are you?" he asked, though he was sure now that he knew.

She turned toward him. For an instant her eyes sparked like twin candle flames. And he saw:

...a leaden rush of river. Candles burning in sardine tins in the grass on the bank. A man lying on his back, moaning as a woman's hand gently fondles his sex.

It is he *who moans.*

The woman moves to straddle him, her orange and lemon peasant skirt belling over her knees, falling to cover his waist. Her fingers release his hardened penis and she shoves her pelvis down, impaling herself on him. He groans, jolts up into her as she brings her hands behind her to the grass.

She rocks upon him, her upper half bare, mottled with strips of candlelight and shadow. He sees her teeth bitten white and sharp into the swelling of her lower lip. He sees the fullness of her breasts swaying. His hands find her knees beneath the gauzy linen of her skirt, but he has no control. It is her need that drives the rhythm.

She releases on him then, in a firecracker string of moans that shudder her thin frame. For a second her movements go languid. He gasps hard; his head thrashes from side to side. His hips thrust and thrust but in this position he can't get deeply enough into her furnace heat to find his own release.

"Please," he begs, "please."

She smiles at him, radiant in sweat.

"Yes, baby," she whispers. Hearing his desire. Responding.

Her hands find his wrists, draw them away from her knees. She rocks forward, sliding down hard on top of him, pushing his hands back onto the grass and holding them there as she begins a slow, sensuous pumping of her hips.

A coral-pink nipple brushes his mouth open. He lifts his head to take it in, his tongue swirling and flicking. She moans, grinding on him now, her movements quickening. He bites at her nipple. Not hard; not gently. Her pace quickens again. And again. Until she shocks wildly up and down on top of him.

His hips begin to flail....

For a second time his release came, driving him to his hands and knees in the dew-wet grass. He gave a low grunt, his muscles gone liquid, his arms trembling.

What was happening to him?

How was it happening to him?

And the woman.

Who?

What?

He lifted his head to find her gone. He'd known she would be.

Soil-musk filled his nostrils. He sneezed. Sneezed again. The tendons in his shoulders felt like stretched piano wires. He slid one knee up, rested his hands there, and used his leg as a lever to heave himself to his feet. Swaying, he stood.

A tangled sheet lay on the bricks before him and he grasped it, lifting it with shaky fingers. Linen. Still holding what felt like warmth. A scent of honeysuckle impregnated the cloth. But there were other odors too, deeper, less pleasant—rubbing alcohol, disinfectant, blood.

An automobile door slammed along River Road.

From beyond the levee came the staccato thrum of a helicopter starting, and the desolate call of a big ship on the Mississippi. He rolled the sheet between his hands, started walking toward his truck, knowing what he would find but needing to play the scene out.

Did that make him crazy?

This night! This whole thing could not be real. But God, he wanted it so—had wanted it and dreamed it for so long. He'd hoped for closure tonight—some kind of closure on guilt and hopeless obsession. Instead he'd found: Hallucinations? Delusions? But they were so intense; he could still feel the pleasure that had torn through him. He could still feel *her*. As he had wished to feel her. If he were crazy, he wasn't ready to seek treatment yet. He kept on walking.

With their moss adornments curling in the breeze, the oaks murmured at his back, as if reluctant to let him go. But he crossed the road to his pickup and got in behind the steering wheel. The overhead light came on, stayed on even after the door was closed. His fingers kneaded the sheet in his lap, and he did not turn at first toward the passenger seat.

"Bring me home," someone said at last.

His fingers stopped working. A shudder wracked him, though through the shudder stabbed a frisson of pleasure.

A fingernail slipped like a raindrop along his cheek then, and he did turn. She sat there—the woman who could *not* be sitting there—looking at him and into him with wide-set eyes that played all the hazel shades of green and blue and grey. The oval of her face was subtly twisted, as if the left cheekbone had healed askew, but she was intensely lovely—like a flawed masterpiece so beautiful that it makes its viewer ache.

The mouth was generous, untouched by injury, with the lower lip fuller than the upper, with both of them blushed faintly with a natural rouge. Tiny dry cracks in the lips set off the fine porcelain paleness of the face. In her hand the woman held one of the orchids that he'd left in the passenger seat. He watched as she lifted the flower and caressed the petals over the heart-line of her mouth.

"Where?" he asked. "Where is home?"

And:

...she leans into him, as if desperate but afraid to close the gap between them. Then she finds the way, her lips warm as they part slightly and she brushes them across his. That contact is feather light but electric, and his hand rises to cup the supple weight of her cheek, his nails sketched along the delicate line of her jaw, molding the petals of the orchid to her skin.

She pulls back for a moment, frowning, studying him intently as if to memorize a face she has dreamed but never seen. Then the color of her eyes deepen and her lids grow heavy with scarcely hidden desire. She moves her mouth toward his again, turning her head to one side, letting her touch-warmed lips skate across his. The tip of her tongue dabs there, sweet and fleeting as mist.

He cannot help but open his mouth under hers. His eyes close as her tongue probes, delving between his lips to meet his own tongue in a brief swirl of heat that turns to hunger. Both his hands cup her face now, his fingers touching flesh, touching petals, craving more.

She presses the kiss, turning her head again, tasting him, working the wet glory of her mouth against his. The faint tick of breathing crackles in the truck, that sound merging with the damp ballet of lips and tongues whispering together.

He opens his eyes....

The orchid fell, fell, fell—out of nothingness to land on the seat. This time he felt no release. The tension of need and want, and of something stronger, ached in him. But it was also outside of himself, centered in the place where she'd been sitting and was sitting no longer. He needed to cry again and could not. He'd known she would be gone if he opened his eyes. He'd tried to keep them closed. But it was too hard to kiss a ghost with your eyes closed.

"No," he corrected himself with a word. She wasn't a ghost. Not quite yet.

He picked up the orchid. Was it only his imagination that painted the petals with a lingering summer warmth? Had to be.

He asked again, into the silent cab of the pickup, "Where is home?" He didn't get an answer. Or expect one.

The sheet that the woman had wrapped herself in was gone from his lap, as the sheaf of hair he'd plucked from the cement drive in the oaks had vanished before. There was nothing of her left here. Not on the road. Or among the oaks. Or in this truck. He was quite sure, in fact, that he'd just lost the last piece of her that had been left anywhere.

That thought burned.

Placing the flower back on the seat, he started the engine and pulled out on River Road, heading toward the city limits of New Orleans. Well before he reached the city line he curved off onto the grounds of Ochsner hospital and found a parking space. He got out of his truck carrying the orchid.

He walked unseeing through the hospital lobby. An elevator let him out on the sixth floor. There were walls of desert tan, others of pastel green. They were meant to sooth and did not. And painted landscapes of vine-covered cottages and quiet ponds did not bring him peace. He barely acknowledged the greetings of the nurses who had grown used to his presence over the past weeks.

The door to room 630 was closed and he pushed it open and stepped inside without knocking. There was no one here to disturb. The blinds were up and he wondered briefly why. Who in this room could appreciate the gray curl of the river behind the trees?

He crossed to the window side of the bed. The beige plastic chair in which he habitually sat was still pulled up next to the dull silver bedrail. He sat again. On the other side of the bed stood a tastefully purple couch, but he had never used it, had never wanted to be too comfortable when he came to this room.

The woman he had run over lay in front of him, with tubes worming down her nostrils and throat, with fluids pump-pumping into her veins. A catheter scribed an "s" across her thin legs before disappearing under the sleeping gown she wore. It wasn't a hospital gown, but something in smooth cotton that he'd bought for her. It was lavender, a color he felt suited her. At one time he'd thought the color pretty. But nothing seemed pretty now.

Except the woman.

She was pale, almost milky, like a fragile work of spun glass nestled in the white sheets. Her hair was Indian jet, lying straight on the pillow. It was shorter on the left than the right. The left side had to grow back. From amid the baroque outlines of the machines that surrounded her came a shush and hum, a language he didn't understand but knew to be important.

The woman did not look as if she had died today.

"Brain dead," the doctors had explained to him.

For months she'd been in a coma and there was hope she would come out of it. The surgeons had fixed most of what was wrong with her on the outside. His insurance had paid some to keep her in this hospital room. He'd paid the rest. Because no one had ever found out who she was or why she'd been on River Road to meet him New Year's Eve. And because of other reasons too.

Not many prayers had come out of him since he was fifteen, but he'd made up for that lack these past few months. He had wanted this woman to open her eyes and smile at him. It hadn't happened. And early, early this morning, before the false dawn, she'd had a stroke and the electrical activity in her brain sank to a flat line that seemed to accuse him.

The ethics committee of the hospital had already met. The

lawyers had seen to having the papers signed. At 8:00 on the coming morning they were going to pull the plug. Then she would, in truth, be a ghost. Other than the doctor, he would be the only person there.

The orchid still dangled between the fingers of his left hand. He reached out with his right and grasped *her* hand. Her skin was cool and sandpaper dry, and he leaned forward to rest his chin on the bedrail above her. It was quite clear to him that he loved this woman. If he'd entertained any doubts, what had happened to him this evening along River Road had obliterated them.

A clinical psychologist would probably tell him that what he'd experienced tonight had been a vivid hallucination compounded out of guilt and stress. In New Orleans, there would be plenty who would give a more occult explanation—a psychic projection by a dying woman, or a spirit knocked free at the moment when he'd hit her, doomed always to haunt that place among the oaks. He didn't like any of those theories; he only wanted her to open her eyes and see him, and she wasn't ever going to.

And he loved her.

The orchid slipped from his fingers.

He loved her.

And watched the flower fall.

He loved her.

Watched it land and bounce once upon her belly.

And:

...the wood-paneled bathroom of a French Quarter hotel. A woman with one cheekbone higher than the other is putting a touch of red on nearly perfect lips as a man watches from the doorway.

He is that man. She is that woman.

The woman smiles at him in the gilt-framed mirror as he steps into the bathroom and runs the knuckles of one hand in a whisper down her back. He kisses the crown of her head, then nuzzles his face into the gleaming mass of her satiny hair. His hands drift lower, coming to rest on the textured cling of her skirt. He presses against her at the waist, his mouth spilling a trail of kisses from her head to her shoulders.

She gasps. Murmurs. "We'll be late for the reception."

"I'm praying so," he says.

She chuckles, starts to turn, but his grip tightens and he holds her there. His breathing hangs heavy in the air, and then there is another sound, the burr of his zipper as he lowers it. The sound is loud as a gunshot in the small room. She shivers.

He brings a hand around her front, fingers nimble as they unbutton the length of her lavender silk blouse. He works the blouse open, reaches inside to free her breasts from the rose lace of her bra.

A thumbnail caresses a ripening nipple. She moans like velvet, her lipstick forgotten in her hand, her body arching forward over the sink, pushing the firm roundness of her bottom against him. He unzips her skirt, lets it slither down her legs to pool on the floor.

His fingers stroke the inside curves of her breasts. Then one hand dips to take the lipstick from her. She purrs deliberately at him, weaving with her bottom against his waist, letting her head dip forward, the hair tumbling in waves over her shoulders.

"Love me," she says.

Her hands clutch at the marble counter; her thighs part with a whisper of friction. He pushes forward from the hips, letting his sex slip between her legs to skate over the petalled gate of her opening.

She swallows hard, breathing in a rush, and he guides the very tip of the lipstick to her belly. He paints a slow swirl there, a crimson ring. Like a lover's bite.

She pants. They shift their weight at the same moment and their bodies slide and fit together. For an instant. Before he pulls back and thrusts again. She follows his rhythm, her eyes closing, her tongue flattening against her teeth.

He drags the lipstick up the length of her belly, pressing harder, bringing it into a scrawl over her breasts, outlining the nipples in brilliant red. His free hand lifts, wraps in her rich mane of hair. He draws her head up, gently, wanting her to look in the mirror as he possesses her, as he moves within her, as he writes in crimson runes across her.

"See how beautiful you are," he says. "How erotic. Can you understand how it is for me? To see you here in silk? To know how close I came to losing you and to want to make you sweat for me? To make you whimper with need for me?"

Her only answer is a low moan that bubbles and breaks in her throat. And she starts to come, jerking forward against the catch of his hand in her hair. He stays with her. Their bodies lock. His heart is like a triphammer.

"I love you," he says, in the instant before his breathing seizes and his own release overpowers him. "Love you. Wife...."

He jerked back from the bedrail, his muscles gone rigid, his pupils wild. *Wife!* He'd said, "wife." But?

Somewhere among all the machinery in the room came a beep. Then another. And more.

The woman in the bed opened her eyes. She picked up the orchid; she squeezed his hand.

"Home," she said, smiling at him.

HEAVEN

The spaceship jarred as it landed. The computer had done its job, had brought me down safely from orbit. But I was half dead, choking for breath, mind spasming from lack of oxygen. The recycler had broken down. Even my space suit was nearly bled dry of air. Somehow, I made it to the airlock.

I didn't know this planet. Was the atmosphere breathable? I had no choice but to find out. The outer hatch opened under my desperate palm. I staggered through, fell to hands and knees, slapped my helmet release.

A breath shuddered into my chest. Warm. Languid. It fed me. My lungs filled with it; my body drank it like nectar. I coughed myself back to life, then forced myself to my feet. The view froze me.

A low mist coiled thickly around my legs, as if I stood on a cloud. But up through the fog thrust metal trees, of copper, black iron, gleaming platinum. Their leaves chimed in a zephyr breeze. Above me, the sky was clear and golden, like melted butter.

In that sky drifted a city of silver. I heard the belling of trumpets, and rising over the city's needle spires came a flock of beings who swept toward me. They were white, blindingly white, with feathered wings.

For an instant I wondered if I had died aboard my ship, or if I lay dreaming with a brain damaged from oxygen loss. But I'd always understood the difference between fantasy and reality, and the reality was that the creatures who dove toward me were angels.They began to sing. My heart swelled with the beauty. I lifted my own voice to join theirs.

The angels swirled before me in diaphanous glory, with luminous eyes honed and piercing. Their wings beat the mist. Their voices lifted higher and higher. For a moment I knew the harmonics of heaven.

Then my own voice faltered; I couldn't match theirs. No human throat could capture this music. No human body could contain it. My chest swelled. My heart hammered and hammered. Again my breath labored. The angels swarmed closer.

I wondered then, why did they point at me as they sang? Why were their sweet lips drawn back over cold smiles? Only when my ears and nose and eyes begin to bleed did I understand. This song was no song at all.

In a rage of laughter, the angels of God tore me apart.

HUNGER

Sunlight fogs the clearing where the dying trees watch; nothing stirs. But the quiet will soon break. Riders are coming from north and south, and before them fly the ravens. The birds come in flocks, light spilling dark from flashing wings. Their cries rasp the sky. A wind moves with them.

The ancient oaks shiver as the black birds settle raucously in their branches. The ravens' agate eyes spark with red as they turn their heads in the sun. The grass stirs now, whispering with gossip as the wind arrives. And there is a rumble in the distance that might be thunder but which the ravens know as the pounding beat of iron-shod hooves.

Up the last hills toward the clearing the riders come, their thunder shaking the earth now, shaking the trees and stirring the birds into a frenzy. Light ripples off armor, off the heads of lances and the bright pennons that snap with eagerness.

The sky roars with sound, then falls nearly silent as the armies draw to a halt facing each other. In the trees, the ravens preside. And the charge comes, as the birds expect. Battle is joined. Carnage riots in the clearing.

First blood soaks the earth, moistens the dry soil. More crimson follows. Buckets of it. It's what the dying oaks have waited for. It's why they've been sending hate over the years into weak human minds, urging them toward war, urging them toward this moment and this place.

Quietly, the oaks begin to bloom. And in the trees' awakening hunger, the ravens are the first to be devoured.

The first. But not the last.

FORGIVEN

it is along the night ways of the water,
where saints ghost through hollow thoughts,
that I stand in temple.
saying the white knuckled rosaries,
teeth locked in the meat of my prayers
while the ashes of my forehead grow cold,
I bow my face.
his words are razors for the licking,
for the blood of the flagellant tongues,
and the crusted rough breads of wickedness
are dipped in the crimson longings of wine.
I kneel my soul.
lay me now to sleep in red-welted dreams.
praise me up to the beaded throne of god,
whose bitter monks are drunk on crosses.
with bright lines of old wounds puckering,
I beg the water.
is there a confessor who is not sold,
who marks not upon his own hands and feet,
who is ripe with the semen of his belief?
I need that one.
it is only when my bones are opened,
when my brain is a drilled hole for light,
that I see the lord.
he has no eyes.
neither is he forgiven.

DEAD TO WRITE

He wore a carapace of bones,
a chill smile in harmony
with his teeth

And echoes were in his eyes,
in the filled membranes
of cold wings

You can't know how he lived
in this unfinished poem

How hard he wanted to write
and no words would come

There were only empty lines
that had been filled up

With Blood.

SHADOW DREAM

Author's Note: the next two stories feature the same character and are written in the same style. Neither is exactly what you'd call a vampire tale, although there are elements of vampirism in them. For some reason, though, they seemed to fit better with this collection than they did with my fantasy collection, Bitter Steel. *"Shadow Dream" was written in 1984 and I consider it to be my second "professional" story. The sequel, "Shadow Wine," has never been submitted. It's not that I consider "Shadow Wine" to be a bad story, but it has always seemed to me to be something of a transitional tale, and when I wrote it I was considering making the* "Shadow Land" *stories into a series. When the chance came to publish this collection, however, I decided that I wanted "Shadow Wine" to be part of it. I guess I've got a soft spot for it. I hope you enjoy.*

The wind came up out of the west, silver with a rain that misted softly across a land of dark fantasy. There were ravens in that land who watched the rain with the eyes of old men, and trees whose crystal leaves chimed as if tears stroked them. The rain fell into rivers that ran in shadows down to the Frozen Sea, and on highways paved with the dust of ancient skulls.

The rain fell, too, on battlements where warriors armored in argent strode, and on towers from whose spires a thousand flags whipped in a thousand hues. It fell on temples raised to dreaming gods and palaces where dragon kings sat brooding, on ruins haunted by the scent of faded wars and on mountains whose eroded faces were those of demons. The rain fell on all corners of the land called Kesh-Kare-Ill, which, perhaps, does not exist except as reflections exist. Jeweled cities stood with their faces to that mist, their streets thronged with people who ignored the drizzle that fell often from the gray skies of Kesh-Kare-Ill. Occasionally, I saw strangers in the crowd. These were mostly wanderers or traders who had crossed the Frozen Sea, or those who had lost their way.

In the marketplaces—beneath blue, and gold, and purple striped awnings that broke the rain—they haggled over the palest of opals and selected pearls without a flaw. They listened in wonder as tiny metal birds chirped stories in their ears, and they tossed stone coins to the blind minstrels who plucked out whispering melodies for them on harps strung with children's tears.

I heard one of the strangers say that he could not stay long, that he must return to the outside world and show men there the treasures of Kesh-Kare-Ill, and I laughed. None have ever been known to leave here. They drink amethyst wines from the vine-yards of Phralis or eat the delicate blooms of the tseatha plant, and they lose their days in cups full of dream and longings for things they cannot name. I should know, for I came as one such wanderer many years ago and have remained. Forever it seems.

A prophet once claimed that only the dead find their way to Kesh-Kare-Ill. But many disputed him. "It is not odd," they said, "that the people are all so very pale here. For the sun is strangely dark and it seems always to be turning late evening. It is not odd that there are no cemeteries here, for many races cremate their dead."

But then, I always wondered why all the songs sung in Kesh-Kare-Ill were songs of lament and dirges to lost souls?

* * * * * * *

Abruptly, I set aside the singing scroll, which has awakened the past for me. The tinkling of its voice chimes on for a moment and then is gone, as the past is gone. I rise and walk across my room to gaze into a mirror at what I have become; my skin is the white of fresh bone and my eyes lie deep beneath their brows. I see that my hair and beard have grown long and are as silver as the rain that falls outside my window, and I do not need the scrolls to help me remember.

In some year whose name is forgotten, a man came to Kesh-Kare-Ill—a lion man, a golden man, a man whose hair flamed like the sun and whose eyes were as deep blue as the mountain lakes of Lochinar, which lies far beyond the Frozen Sea. He crossed that sea alone, on a ship with grey sails that slid on diamond runners over the dark ice, and reached a quiet harbor to the north of the land.

Mountains stood blocking his way, but they did not stop him. His first assault carried him up to their needle spires, and his second brought him down the far slopes amid the rumbling echoes of his passage. No one remembered when those peaks had last been scaled.

The man traveled on foot until he reached the lower hills, and there, in a silent amphitheater of stone, he trapped an emerald stallion with fanged eyes and broke him to his will. There was blood on this man and heat lightning in his swift movements, and blood, too, was on the broadsword that hung over his shoulder. That blade had been recently cleaned and sharpened—as if from a battle—but when one looked with the eyes of the past the stains were still there. He rode from that place on his stallion's flying hooves, and like a dagger he clove into the heart of Kesh-Kare-Ill. The hoof beats rang behind him and shattered the silence.

Where he entered the land it was not far to Timorii the Jaded, Timorii the City of Solitude, which lies along the Road of Sighs just past the dolmens dedicated to the melancholy god Sephraell. With an iron dirk he carved his name on one of those standing stones. It is still there for I have recently seen it—Chalice Tenethosse, Chalice Goldenhorn.

Chalice came to Timorii in the cyan evening with a storm as

his mantle. Massive clouds boiled and heaved, vomiting darkness and savage lightning that ran purple to the ground. And on that day it rained as it had never rained in Kesh-Kare-Ill—in rivers, and seas, and oceans that shattered the crystal forests into myriad fragments and washed like a tide over the walls of all the cities in the land.

The people of Timorii, accustomed only to mists, fled inside their black domes, and everywhere the echoes came of slamming doors and shuttering windows. Even warriors shivered in their armor, and drew their weapons closer, and caressed their steel.

Chalice sat his horse outside the open gate of the city and smiled as the rain plastered his red-blond hair to his skull and water sluiced in a torrent from his harsh features. He stood in his stirrups and shook a fist at the storm and laughed in booming notes to rival the thunder.

I remember that when he came through the gates and entered the city, the streets were lorn, wet, and drifting with shadows flung down like gauntlets by the hurtling storm. Chalice moved along those broad avenues like a predator, a single warrior, rippling scarlet. Straight on he rode, toward the palace of the Chalk King, and guards moved with swords and bronze bucklers and would have barred his path.

Blades rasped from jeweled scabbards and flashed violent—and violet with lightning—but Chalice did not stop. He drove his jade stallion forward and rode them down, rode them all down in a cold dream of steel that left sobbing screams dying behind him in the dusk.

So the barbarian came to Timorii, hot with passion, driven by lusts, and later that night, as the storm worshipped the earth, Chalice stood on the highest tower of the Palace of Raptors, shouting his name at the city and demanding allegiance. At his feet lay the dead and broken body of the Chalk King, and the chained loveliness of the queen who would live now as his slave.

There had never been such a man in Kesh-Kare-Ill, a man of demon strengths and ripping eyes, and the melancholy warriors flocked to his banner. Armies rose overnight to make war in his name, and they carried the torch of conquest to the Frozen Sea, and the Hollow Lands, and even unto the gates of fabled Tolembarach at the edge of the Plain of Sorrows.

Always those armies rode beneath the banner of the golden horn on the scarlet field, and always they won: at Djinn Valley and Thorn Ridge, and at half a hundred other battlefields without names. In an instant it seemed, Chalice's will charged the blood and passions of a hundred thousand men, and in that one short moment Kesh-Kare-Ill fell and the soul of Chalice Goldenhorn was nearly lost.

Only at Tolembarach was he defied, and he raged there and swore to tear the city stone from stone and give it to the sea. But he did not.

On a twilight evening, while the siege fires played like fire elementals across the Plain of Sorrows, the young queen of Tolembarach came to the walls and gave strength to her people. Chalice Goldenhorn saw her there, with her pale skin, and her dark hair strung with pearls, and a gossamer gown that floated like a rapture around her slim form. He saw her and loved her then. And forever.

For her, he spared the city that had defied him. For her, he turned away from his anger and from the conquest that had given him an empire. His armies melted away; his banner fell and was buried in dust. Swords rusted in their sheaths and shields lay broken and forgotten on ancient fields of battle. The warhorses died and the ruins of empire sang lost songs of past glories whenever the wind blew through them. And he loved her then, and forever.

For a thousand years they reigned in Tolembarach—golden king and pale queen—and it seemed for a time as if summer had come to the autumn land. One could stand on the walls of the city and look down on fields of grain ripening perpetually amid dusky yellow sunshine. In the evening, warm zephyrs beat back the mistral winds of the mountains, and hoarfrost no longer formed on the streets during the blackness of night.

For the first time in Kesh-Kare-Ill's history, children sang songs that were not full of weeping. But time does not stop, and even a thousand years seem ephemeral when they are over.

Perhaps it was the coming of a storm like that which had harbinged his arrival at Timorii that shattered the spell, or perhaps it was the sound of the too lonely wind that blows always in the empty towers of Tolembarach that at last broke the shadow dream. Chalice awoke one day with his love beside him and found the castle paved with dust, the precious tapestries dimmed and torn. The winged spiders had come and spun their webs so thick in the room where he lay with his queen that they hung like cerements from the marble ceiling.

In horror, Chalice gazed upon the dead and blackened flower petals that lay scattered across the tiled floor. Only last night they had been freshly gathered and strewn to make a carpet for the feet of his lover.

He turned to her then and touched her shoulder beneath the rotted purple silk that had once draped their bed. She was only an empty corpse's shell, and her mummified flesh crumbled to powder beneath his hand. He stood, crying out, her beauty running like dust through his grasping fingers, and for the first time he looked down on himself naked and saw the great savage wound in his chest that had taken his life so many centuries ago. And he knew.

Only the dead find their way to Kesh-Kare-Ill.

* * * * * * *

Long years have passed since that day and Kesh-Kare-Ill lies empty. Its dead are no longer remembered in the outer world and even shades have no existence without memories.

I remain—alone—and I do not even know why. My hair is the color of frost now and my skin has the texture of faded parchment. In the mirror, I can barely see my pale blue eyes lying deep within their sockets. I am the emperor Chalice Goldenhorn and am king over nothing.

Yet, I remember a woman who once I knew, and I loved her then, and will love her forever:

Chimera. Chimera.

SHADOW WINE

A dead man's reflection lived in the empty depths of my wine grail. It looked up at me with faded blue eyes that were just like mine, that wept just like mine. I believe the lich wished to be my friend, but I would not let him. I did not want him. I covered his face with black wine and drank once more, deeply.

Outside my fortress at Tolembarach, the twilight mistral began to play. I heard its sound skirling around my windows as its cold seeped into the room where I sat. It seemed almost as if it were winter, but there are no seasons in Kesh-Kare-Ill. Day follows day and they are all the same, all filled with the shadow sun that gives no warmth, the shadow wind that stirs chill memories.

My name is Chalice Goldenhorn and once I was emperor in Kesh-Kare-Ill. Once I was loved, by a people, and by a woman. Sometimes when lost in my cups I see the ruins of all that I possessed in the lees of the wine. I hear the harsh flutings of combat in the scraping breeze. I hear the cheering throngs who call my name. I touch the lips of my dark haired queen.

But those days are passed. There are no wars left; no warriors remain. And the throngs have gone as my love has gone—into dust. For these are the Shadow Lands where spirits dwell for that infinite time between death and the final dissolution of the soul. Only now, all the souls except for mine are missing. I do not know why. The city stands around me; the streets still seem to echo with passing footsteps. But only the ghosts of the ghosts still belong here.

I have considered the possibility that I am mad and that this is all just dreams. But I do not believe that. I see too well what I have become, ancient and ephemeral, my flesh grown so translucent that when I hold my hand up to the stars I catch their bitter cold gleam through the milk-white of my skin. Soon, perhaps, I too will fade away and be gone. Often I have hoped that it comes quickly. Wine and memories make poor companions for lonely nights.

Despaired of thoughts, I rose and staggered away, carrying my bottle of courage. I walked lorn halls and cried cold tears that dissipated in the air before reaching the floor. I do not know what impulse pushed me into the corridors that led into the depths of Tolembarach—it had been long since my feet trod there—but perhaps there were gods who drew me, or maybe demons.

Below the city stood an amphitheater where my love and I had wed, and where I had laid aside my sword for the last time. I had never before returned to the place, but now, drawn by nameless longings, I entered the room where I had been prepared for the marriage ceremony. It had once been sumptuously furnished, as befitted one who was to become an emperor. Now the tapestries and mosaics hung in tatters and the rugs were rotted away. The sight filled me with self-pity.

I stood there a long time, my mind aching with memories, and at last turned to go. Then a voice, or something *like* a voice, whispered in my ear, though the room was empty. I could find no reason for the disturbance and turned once more to go, and again a sound—like words in the language of sabers—sliced sharp into my awareness. I searched the room carefully but found nothing. Except. On one wall hung my ancient broadsword, unsheathed. It alone of all this world still gleamed as if new. But now it bore a shine that did not seem due to polished steel, and the black runes etched into the blade's surface writhed like smoke.

Fascinated, I went over to the wall and stood staring into the vast depths of the sword. In its mirrored surface I saw the old man I'd become, and rage blossomed in me. I hurled the bottle I carried against the wall. It shattered, and the dark wine ran down like blood over the gray stone.

With hot violence seething in my veins, I reached up and took the sword. The hilt fitted perfectly into my fists. I lashed out with the brand and crushed a suit of crystal armor that stood nearby. I spun the blade in my hands and hacked through a mahogany table. The berserk came upon me. I leaped from the room, hearing the roar of spectators, as if the amphitheater was filled with wild crowds.

A man stood before me on the raked sand. He was tall and barbaric. His hair flamed red-gold and his eyes were a deep, killer's blue. He wore no armor, only a linen loincloth, and scars arced across his chest and shoulders. But he carried a sword, a twin to the one that filled my own hand.

The warrior came for me and I met him in the center of the arena. Steel screeched as our weapons met. His movements were shockingly swift, but somehow I matched him, and then surpassed him. His face showed surprise when I began to drive him back, but no fear. Three times he tried to force his way past me and three times I beat down his guard and turned him away. Then his back was to the wall, with blood streaming down his chest and legs from a dozen sword cuts. He raised his weapon as I prepared to finish him and saluted me with the steel.

"To you is the victory," he said, and he turned into smoke that blew past me, and into me.

I leaned on my sword, panting from exertion. The arena around me seemed strangely silent of a sudden, and when I looked up no one was there. Then I realized who I had fought.

I raised my sword and looked once more into its surface. A young man's face looked back at me, a man with red-gold hair and savage beard, a man with golden skin and deep blue eyes, a man who stroked his blade with one scarred hand. In his chest, in *my* chest, there was another scar, as if from a wound freshly healed. I remembered the lance which had made that wound; I remembered that I had died from it. And, laughing, I strode from that place.

The singing scrolls speak of many lands that lie beneath the shadow sun. Why had I not thought of them before? They carry names like Tanthera, Laer-Dane, Jykastra, Changrillmir. They remained to be conquered. And in the end I would find my way home to Lochinar, the land of my birth, home through all the terrors the shadow worlds could stab at me, and through all the monsters in my own soul.

Only for a moment did I hesitate, my thoughts turning to my lost queen. I went and gathered her dust into a vial to carry with me, and then strode away.

GOODIES

Stark and black, the oaks rose through the morning's ghostly fog, Spanish moss dripping from their limbs like the hair of drowned corpses. Beneath the oaks, twelve year old Emmy stopped as a sound whispered along the trail before her.

"That you, Mom?"

It was just like her mom to try and scare her.

"Mom?"

There wasn't any answer and Emmy doubted it had been her mother anyway. The breeze would have brought Mom's scent. She hitched her heavy bag higher on one thin shoulder and walked on. Nothing jumped her, though she was ready for it.

Then she was free of the oaks and stalking through a meadow toward her grandmother's cabin. It was brighter here, the fog lifting. Her feet swished in thick, wet grass. A spider web fingered her face. She brushed it away as she knocked on grandmother's door.

"Come in," a guttural voice called.

The door creaked opened. Night lingered within and Emmy flicked on the flashlight that she carried in one pocket of her red parka.

Grandma's house was an abattoir.

Emmy's eyes widened. There were more bodies than last time. Some were alive, or semi-alive. Every one of them stunk with rot.

"Well come on, Dear," the voice called again, impatiently.

Emmy started forward between two chained rows of drooling

forms. Hungry moans roiled the air. She ignored them. Broken fingered hands grasped at her. She ducked them, her feet kicking tibias and ribs from her path, some cracked and bleached white, some...meaty.

Just past the zombies, Grandmother's door stood open. Grandma lay on the bed amid quilts and pillows. She was still in wolf form.

"You brought the stuff?" Grandma demanded.

"I brought it," Emmy said.

She sat her bag on the bed and Grandma jerked it away with taloned hands and ripped it open. Livers and hearts and links of intestines spilled out like a miser's hoard, but Grandma had eyes for only one thing, a jar of rare delicacies. She grabbed it, tore off the lid and dipped within to pull out a pinkish, cauli-flower-sized lump.

"Ah," she sighed, popping the thing between her teeth. "Melts in your mouth." She reached for another.

Emmy frowned. "I thought you liked hearts best, Grandma. Mom only sent four baby brains."

Grandma chuckled, stroked Emmy's head with clawed fingers.

"Tastes change," she said, grabbing another tidbit.

Emmy frowned again, and a sudden gasp spilled from her lips.

Grandma heard the gasp and turned bloodshot eyes accus-ingly upon her granddaughter. The last brain was chewed mush in her mouth.

"What, child?"

"That bite on your shoulder, Grandma! Where did you get it?"

Grandma smiled, with teeth that could crush spines.

"Just a scratch, Dearie. Come, give Grandma a hug."

Shaking back her hood, Emmy drew the nickel-plated .357 from the pocket of her red parka. She knew where Grandma's bite had come from. Grandma had gotten careless with a zombie.

With a howl, Grandma leaped from the bed, her eyes

screaming hunger, her mouth screaming, "brains, brains!"

Emmy pulled the trigger. There was only one cure for what ailed Grandma.

A silver bullet.

Through the head.

DEATH IS

Death is a wild and beautiful lover, pale as the earliest slice of morning. She is a dark-eyed harlequin of evil intent, oiled and perfumed like an exquisite machine—with the lips that Satan dreamed of in his long fall to hell. And always she is the sweetest razor, a rotted angel, all tattooed venom in her cloak of bones.

God, I adore her.

BLUE SOUL

if i were the blue soul of god,
the ancient white heart of heaven,
i would have seen the hunger
that burns in your wine throat.
i would have been the ghosts
whose blood you worship.
and if you preyed to me
in the alien words of lost children,
if you gave me sweet succor
for my innocent lips,
for the scars of my life,
i would claim you mine.
written in fog,
sung in the cold whisper of winter,
i would claim you mine,
and there would be no end
to our love.

ROTTED ANGELS

Rotted angels
swallow oblivion
in wine and sweat
and the odor
of a dark embrace

ROTTED ANGELS 2

They dance in dust and dead leaves,
in the fall of rain
rushing to earth.
They watch from beds of shadow,
rotted angels
with hearts in their mouths.
And I hear them speak,
I hear them whisper,
from all my hollow places,
in the language of scorpions.

LILY WHITE AND RED

The woman walks in a desert turned bronze by the afternoon sun. Her gown is white, her hair pale gold. The day is cool, with the sky clear and a taste of winter chill in the soughing wind. She walks a long way. In time she comes to a ruined city where the last wall standing holds once-bright murals that have faded and worn to shadows. She passes through the memory of an ancient gate.

Tool-worked stones lie scattered along her path, some of them the remnants of statues, others of temples and palaces. Broken fountains pour only dust. She follows what must once have been a road while evening gathers around her like a cloak. When night falls, it finds her standing beside an open well whose dark depths gleam with phosphorescence. Lilies are carved in the granite of the well's rim.

The woman's *name* is Lily, and though the world seems empty around her, she knows it is not. Above her, the stars are coming swiftly into the sky, as if myriad eyes are opening to watch her.

She sits in the dust, facing the well with her back to a leaning pillar. When the rising moon touches her with its glamour, she hears a whisper, like leather over rock. And she smells the perfume of crushed Amaryllis petals.

In the next moment, a man is there, at the lip of the well. He rises out of a whirl of dust that carries the scent of rains and pollen overlying a hint of rot. His body is a mahogany curve in the moonshine. His hair hangs long past his shoulders and is a dreadlocked black. He does not speak to her in words, but his fingers weave runes in the air that glitter.

"I am many," Lily translates.

It is not clear whether Lily understands the runes or whether the man's mind speaks the meaning directly to hers. But more runes fall from the man's fingers, and, as if commanded, the woman rises from her place and moves forward to brush her palm across his lips, lips seemingly far too lush to exist in this barren landscape. The man takes her hands in his, cups them as if they are a sparrow with broken wings. He leans to kiss her. She tastes his mouth. And it is bitter. She tastes his need. And it is far beyond sweet.

The ruins vanish; the city's walls and buildings rise anew. Around Lily and her darkling lover, a palace crystallizes where lamps burn like gold. Beneath multiple gleamings, the two dance. Laughter riots. A feast is spread before them. They eat of pomegranates and dragon fruit. They spice their tongues with fennel. And as the lamps burn down they nestle in furs and silks and Lily fucks her lover against the world. No thought of death can touch them.

But dawn is coming and is not kind.

As morning light fingers its way to earth, the city's outlines begin to waver. The man awakens, gazes down upon his Lily. Somehow in the sharing of bodies his plans for her have altered. He is sated, though he did not drink that which he had thought to drink. He thinks now to take her to his dark well, where they can entwine in soft shadows during heated day. He shakes her shoulder.

She opens her eyes—clotted eyes—and the man begins to scream. He tries to scramble away, and Lily's hands, which were like sparrows last night are like hawks today. She drags him beneath her and her mouth finds his. She tears away his full lips, tears away his tongue. She discovers his throat and delights there. His screams strangle in a flood of gore.

Lily floats to her feet, her ivory gown dyed to scarlet. The man lies in pieces, with legs and arms separated from head and torso. But he is not dead. Blood still flushes from him, as if he is a fountain of red. For he is a vampire and he is many.

The ruby serum filters along the mosaics of the floor, wicks its way up the chinks in the walls. It fills them, steadies them. It pours out to paint the streets beyond. The city stands. Even against the sun.

Lily finds her throne room. She caresses her chair of fangs and seats herself amid pillows sewn from the emptied skins of her victims. There are many pillows, and there will be more. In time, the strength of her vampire lover will fail and he will cease to bleed. Her city will return to ruins. The scarlet of life will fade, and the scent of death and decay will attract another vampire, another source of blood.

And in white, Lily will walk again.

IN THE SHADOW OF THE ROSE

Prologue

Two roses bloomed in the cold desert—one black, one pale—their scent calling on the wind. Two warriors answered, from the east in silver, from the west in jet. Their mounts were the colors of chalk and of coal. Broadswords flamed—dazzling the skies—and the warhorses charged, laying waste to dust. Amid the flashing of armor and the stride of the horses, the champions came together. Silver blade met sable. Steel rang, screaming. And they passed.

Hooves danced amid spurts of dust as the horses circled and came together again. The weapons sang, throwing echoes into the distance. One horse stumbled. The silver warrior dropped his guard as he reached for the reins of his falling charger. A black sword caught him in the chest, pierced the armor, and came away red.

The echoes died in the sound of thunder. Clouds stalked greyly across the sky, casting violet spears at the earth. The petals of the white rose fell and drifted away like snow. The black rose cried, its tears scarlet.

I.

A man and a horse came into the wastes. There was cold with them, enough to turn the breath from their mouths to smoke, and the sun gave no warmth from behind its shield of clouds. Drizzle fell from those clouds, turning to ice where it struck the ground, and the travelers were looking for shelter. It was a lifeless plain where they searched, a vast wilderness planted only with boulders. Yet they found a place near twilight, a dolmen of gray rock raised to someone long dead.

The man threw up camp where the stone broke the wind and rain. He built a fire with wood he had carried with him and ate from his meager supply of bread and meat. The horse, too, fed, then turned its back to the wind as horses have done since time began. The man sat alone and stirred the fire with a stick, sipping occasionally from a skin of bitter wine. After a while, he curled up in his blankets and slept.

When dawn was still far away a sound came across the wasteland and woke the man. He started and sat up, hand grasping at the saber by his side. The horse snorted in fear and the man realized the strange sound was only a wolf crying at the sky. Yet he wondered, not without a chill, what a wolf would find to eat in a land such as this.

Unable to return immediately to sleep, the man rose and walked from the dolmen's shadow onto the plain, his boots crunching a thin layer of ground-ice. The drizzle had stopped and the clouds were breaking. The moon hung bright and silver in the dark sky, flirting with the wisps that remained. The ancient stone monument bulked hugely at the man's back; the breeze tugged at his hair, carrying iciness in its fingers. He shivered and turned back toward his bed, and a glint of captured moonlight stabbed his eyes.

Curious, he walked toward the glint, nearly stumbling over a skeleton left from some forgotten battle. It lay like a wrecked ship in the sand, the shining armor it had once worn turned dark with age and rust. A spider had spun silk between the ribs and crystals of frost were laced like diamonds through the tracery of the web. Something metallic lay beneath the outstretched bones of the hand.

The man went to one knee and scraped away the dirt, gasping when his brushing fingers revealed the rune-covered hilt of a sword. The blade came easily from the dried soil, leaving its grave behind. It was a broadsword, of a style used long ago, but time and the desert had not etched its surface. Though it looked like silver, it stroked like steel. The edge still held its sharpness.

The cold weapon warmed quickly in his grasp, as if drinking heat from his body. A tingle tightened his scalp—a premonition perhaps—and he started to return the sword to its rest. But the moon chose that moment to smile and the weapon turned to beauty as it cast back the light. Incised with exquisite care along the hilt and flat of the blade lay the image of a rose.

Entranced, the man carried the weapon to his camp, failing to notice the horse shy away when he entered the firelight. He *did* notice when the breeze carried a faint sound to his ears, like distant hooves pounding. He thought it was loneliness playing its tricks and he soon slept again, only to find his dreams disturbed by pale horses and warriors with haunted eyes.

II.

The wanderer had broken his fast by the time the sun opened its lone eye, and he rode out soon afterward, his new sword hanging at his back. The horse had seemed uneasy this morning and he'd had to fight it to mount. But at least the skies were clear, the wind only a little cold as it followed them. It was a good day to ride, and another seemed to agree. Behind him throughout the morning he heard the shout of hooves. He no longer doubted their existence, as he had last night, and he wondered who trailed him.

He had come far, this man named Jaal Harkest, and, young

as he was, there were lands where they would hunt him as an outlaw for the coins his scalp would bring. This was not such a land. To this place he had ridden quietly, for miles through an empty world. In the north, in far Teshrakana, he had found this waste marked on a map. Before that he had known of it only from the vellum-bound journal in his saddlebags, the journal left for him by his mother, whom he had never met.

Putting thoughts of his mother's writing aside, Jaal stopped for a noon meal where he could be easily seen by whoever dogged his tracks. No one came to visit, however, and after an hour passed without incident he rode on. The sound of hooves soon joined him again.

III.

The evening came swiftly it seemed, but Jaal welcomed it. He was tired and lightheaded, anxious to stop. The rose-engraved sword made a heavy weight across his back, pulsing hot on his skin. His hands shook, at least in part from the strain of being followed. Sometimes the hoof beats would sound so close, as if right at his heels, but no one was there when he turned to look. And the sound would stop.

Jaal camped near a jumble of stones and built a fire. He badly wanted a cup of Kaf and had just dumped the ground beans into boiling water when he heard hooves approaching and stood up. It was still light enough to see his pursuer, a single rider who topped a narrow ridge not thirty yards away and halted. The rider wore silver armor with a full-faced helm, and sat astride a stallion as pale as snow.

Jaal drew his saber against attack, but when none came he remounted his horse and started it toward the stranger. He would find what the fellow wanted, and if it were a fight then he would be happy to oblige. With a start, Jaal noted the sudden emptiness on the ridge above him, where seconds before a horseman had sat. He raced up the short slope to look off the other side.

The plain stretched for miles, and was empty. Jaal felt a curling of hair on his neck, and a chill that was not all from the wind.

Back at his camp, Jaal drank Kaf and sat in silence. The runes of the ancient broadsword sang in the breeze and drew the fire's smoke. Sleep was slow in coming that night, and was not restful when it arrived.

IV.

By dawn, Jaal was ill, his flesh hot and his mouth dry. Nausea lurched in his belly. He had a cup of cold Kaf and pushed on, seeing mountains to the south and reaching for them as a drowning man reaches for shore. Throughout the day the strange hooves rang behind him, growing louder and stronger as he grew weaker. Again and again he turned to face his pursuer, only to find nothing. He was driven now, and knew it. His reasons for coming to this waste were abandoned. He wanted only to be away.

The broadsword hanging over his shoulder was a piece of what Jaal wanted to escape, and he took it off once, thinking to discard its weight. He did not. The hilt pulsed under his hand and he could almost hear the runes thrumming faintly in the breeze, the sound hovering on the edge of meaning, like a language learned in childhood and not quite forgotten. It made him think about how much the blade would be worth in the south to those who collected the old artifacts, and he put the weapon back over his shoulder and booted the horse forward.

Exhaustion finally brought Jaal to camp, both his own exhaustion and that of his horse. Neither could eat, and their sleep that night was disturbed by visions. Jaal fought with things he could not name, drowned to the sound of their laughter, screamed at their flaming eyes, fell from beneath their wings. The sweat of fear soaked man and horse alike, and then froze as the cold grew in the dark stillness. Even the fire seemed to hate that stillness, and drew in on itself until the only brightness in the camp was the diamond length of the ancient sword. There was no heat in that brightness, but there was a very old anger.

V.

The gelding had broken its tether and was gone when morning came. Its fleeing stride was long and Jaal knew it must have been afraid and running. He had no energy left to worry about a horse's fears, though. His own were enough to choke him.

He let the saddle lie, but took up his blankets, his saber, and his water and began to walk. Once again he tried to leave the broadsword, but the swift breeze played along the lines of the engraved rose as if the blade called to him. That call was not to be ignored, and he had gone scarcely twenty paces before returning to take up the ancient thing again. Thoughts of gold consoled him, that and dreams of the dark-eyed women who would come with the coins.

In the day's heat, however, it was not long before even thoughts were gone and Jaal just reeled on across the desert, edging slowly into delirium. He lost even the concept of time and did not know how far he had traveled when a stench soured his nostrils and brought his head around. He thought it was something dead, but what he saw was the stranger who followed him on a pale horse. Jaal was close enough now to notice many things about the warrior he had not seen before, the empty scabbard at the figure's side where a sword had once hung, the archaic designs of the armor and saddle, the helmet forged in the likeness of an amber-eyed dragon.

The stranger held out his fist to Jaal and opened it. In the palm lay a white rose in full bloom. Slowly, while the outlaw watched, the gauntleted fist closed over the delicate petals. Slowly, the blossom crushed beneath that grip. Jaal scented the flower's dying perfume and saw blood run from the warrior's hand. The destroyed bloom fell on the dirt. The bloody silver fist went up and pulled back the dragon helmet. Behind that helm coiled black sockets in a hydrocephalic cranium, and the teeth filling the mouth were stained a permanent red.

The outlaw's heart fluttered; his eyes burned. He spun about and fled. But Jaal Harkest was a brave man and did not run far. After a dozen strides he slowed, then stopped and drew his saber. He would not run, not even from a dead man. But as he turned to face his tormenter a cold wind raced by him and away. There was nothing else.

Abruptly, the strength went out of Jaal's legs and he sat down hard, laughing wildly in release. Of course he had not seen what he thought he had. The dead had no need of horses, and roses did not bleed. It was a trick of the desert and of fever. A mirage. He'd heard of such things occurring in the wastes. It was even to be expected, and he kept repeating that to himself as he got up and walked on toward the mountains.

VI.

Dusk found Jaal staggering into what he thought were the foothills of the Sentai Range. A stammer of thunder had grown steadily behind him for hours and he looked for a place to wait out the coming storm. He looked for a place, too, where he could stop running. In the end, there had been no way to convince himself that he had seen a mirage. He trusted his senses, which meant he was being driven by something unnatural living in this waste. He would not be driven further.

It was at just that moment, as if intended to give the lie to his thoughts, that a surge of lightning rippled down to earth, freezing the night into a momentary sculpture. In the baleful light, Jaal realized at last how *much* he had been driven. The mountains toward which he had traveled for days were gone. Before him on the sand stood the dolmen where he had found the rose-engraved broadsword.

If the realization that he'd been traveling in a circle was meant to break him, it failed. His spine stiffened with anger and he drew his saber. In his weakened state it took both Jaal's hands to lift the blade, but the very act calmed his heart and his grip steadied.

"Come on!" he shouted at the night. "Come and end the farce." Then a half smile played around his mouth. *If you can*, the smile said.

The answer to Jaal's challenge was a scream of pounding hooves on hard packed desert soil. The sound came from behind him, and he spun around just as the lightning flashed again, its cyan veins writhing like worms in the sky. Out of the flash bloomed a pale shadow on a ghost-colored mount, and a gauntleted fist slapped at Jaal's head with a enough force to crush the fragile shell of his skull. The outlaw dropped beneath the blow and slashed at the legs of the charging war-horse. His blade met resistance but evoked no sound of agony, and the destrier thundered by unchecked.

Again the charge came. Again Jaal met it, swinging up and across with all his strength. He missed, though he should not have, and something cold and hard buffeted his shoulder, hurling him from his feet.

Jaal pushed back to his knees, heard the sound of a charge but saw nothing. Then hellish lightning sword-stroked the apparently empty night, and the crunch of thunder massacred any sound but its own. His eyes and ears temporarily numbed, Jaal felt a hand clutch his wrist and draw him to his feet. The grip was preternaturally strong, and Jaal released the saber as his wrist bones ground together in agony.

In the next flare of lightning, the outlaw saw clearly what had followed him. Dark orbits stared from a grotesquely enlarged skull, their depths empty of all but sorcerous gleamings. Below those holes were yellowed nares and the oval of a mouth where dwelt a black tongue and crimson teeth. Hollow laughter curdled like sour wine in Jaal's blood, and the youth heard his death in that laughter, saw his own sword drawn back for a thrust into his belly. He felt the overwhelming presence of evil and screamed, but the scream was of rage rather than fear.

Savagely, Jaal drew the ancient broadsword from over his shoulder and struck at the arm holding him. The edge met resistance and sheared through. The argent warrior staggered back, the empty sleeve of its armor pouring dust. The grip on Jaal's wrist fell away. A silver gauntlet dropped at his feet, its fingers spasming on the outlaw's saber.

The outlaw raised the broadsword for another blow, but the sorcerer's empty sockets sparked suddenly with bright detonations of mauve, ochre, and anil. The flashing lights caught at Jaal, ate at him, held him still. Against his will's orders, his legs took a step forward, then another, his boots dragging like chains. The broadsword leaped in his grip, turning in his hands until it faced toward his chest. He fought to alter its course, but all his strength meant nothing. The sword was going to kill him, with his own fingers on the hilt.

The pressure eased abruptly as the lich heard something that distracted it. Jaal heard it too, the susurration of sand grains slipping and sliding against one another. Both looked toward the sound, toward the dolmen that had marked Jaal's entrance into the waste and which had been about to mark his exit. The huge stone had been standing dark and alone. Now it gleamed like alabaster and was accompanied by twin spires forming out of spinning sand.

In another instant, the silicate towers congealed into forms that resembled blooming roses. One was black, the other silver. Jaal had come into this waste to find just such markers. They were recorded in his mother's journal. Then a black horse came from between the rose towers as if fleshed from the night. A black armored rider sat its saddle. The storm died overhead.

The silver warrior swayed at sight of the rider, as if its bones had turned suddenly to reeds, and the mental vise that gripped Jaal's will released like bursting swamp bubbles. The outlaw responded quickly, lunging forward to drive the broadsword deep into the thin brigandine armor defending the rib cage of his foe. The only result was a backhand slap that sent Jaal spinning to earth.

An armored boot stomped down at Jaal's head, but the outlaw avoided it as he rolled to his feet and slashed the sword at the creature's midsection. He hoped to cut the thing in half, but the skeleton warrior was just fast enough to dodge. Jaal bore in, pressing a temporary advantage, and a silver hand opened and cast a fistful of angry red wasps into his face. Jaal was stung once, twice, before the wasps flashed into crimson dust. Behind him amid the sand towers, Jaal heard the black rider shouting incantations. His enemy's sorcery was being countered.

The lich realized the same thing and used its remaining hand to scoop up Jaal's saber from the dirt. Jaal smiled. Few could match him with a blade, and he did not think a being who had always depended on sorcery would be one of them.

The ancient broadsword was heavy, but it danced in Jaal's hand like a wand. In moments the wizard's tarnished armor hung in threads. An instant later, no head rested on the skeleton's shoulders. It lay on the sand at Jaal's feet, and the outlaw watched as the glittering light faded to cold darkness in the pitted eyes. Before even the last flicker was gone, Jaal felt a presence at his shoulder and turned. The black horse waited there, its rider covered in armor and motionless in the saddle.

"I thank you for your service in my cause," Jaal said.

"And I for yours," the rider added quietly.

The voice was a woman's, and Jaal's eyes widened.

The black warrior dismounted to stand over the fallen sorcerer, and as she stood she loosed the straps of her helmet. Jaal was afraid of what the helm might reveal when it was removed, but the face that turned toward him was clothed in flesh and in the sockets were human eyes, full of pity and of pain. Jaal wondered who the pain was for.

"Centuries ago," the woman said, gesturing to the bones at her feet, "this man was a sorcerer grown strong in evil. His name was Naidir. It was told by a seeress at his birth that he would die at the hands of his brother. At fifteen, Naidir murdered his brother. Even I could not kill him after that, though I stopped him for a time. A long time. I was his mother. And I am your mother too, though I left you when you were a child."

Jaal had known what the woman was going to say before she said it, but that didn't stop the words from scourging him, or hope from leaping into his throat.

"At least now I've found you," he said.

New pain multiplied in her eyes. "No," she said. "Now you have lost me."

Jaal stepped forward, a question forming on his lips. But in that instant a wind swirled around him and he found himself stepping toward a crumbling pillar of dust. He reached a hand, felt it scoured with sand. The wind fell and the night grew still.

A faint perfume tickled the young outlaw's nostrils, and he looked down at the dead sorcerer's skull. An ebon flower grew from one empty, staring socket, and in the shadow of that rose liquid beads of black and silver glistened on the ivory, as if two sets of tears had fallen there and joined. Some distant voice whispered in Jaal's ear, but he could not be sure of the words. Then he threw down the ancient broadsword and strode away.

LOVERS

They were running, moving swiftly through the rain-wet streets of Deerhaven, she in front and he behind, and he wanted very much to catch her. He needed to catch her. The muscles bunched and rolled beneath his skin, and the click of feet on pavement hammered out a rhythm that pounded through into his brain. And she was so close, running in the midst of a thousand different odors, the smell of heat that was burned by her body, the smell of her breath as it spilled behind her. It only made him want her all the more and he picked up the pace.

He absolutely had to catch her.

The chase had started in an empty lot behind the old lumberyard and it seemed they had been running for hours, though it had not been nearly so long. It was only that his life had become a kind of movement, a flowing river of scent that was heavy and wet, a blur of streetlights that glinted from metallic looking puddles. There was, as well, the beginning of pain, a cooking in his chest as if someone had peeled back his ribs and fired up a barbecue inside.

And still she was strong, racing smoothly and evenly ahead of him, never out of his sight, never within his reach. The part of him that had not yet reverted fully back to his animal instincts knew he should have caught her by now. He should have had her before they'd gotten out of the weed strewn lots around the lumberyard and into the more brightly lit streets of the town. Even in a place as small as Deerhaven, Arkansas, and even at 2:30 at night, there was too much chance of being seen. But maybe that had been her hope, that he'd back off rather than follow her into the open. If so, she had badly underestimated her hold over him. He would follow her into hell now, if that was what it took to catch her.

Then, as if his conscience was punishing him for ignoring it, a car went splashing by, its windows streaming with rain. The vehicle's driver stared and stared, until she nearly took out a fire hydrant with the front of her Buick. By then the two were past her, racing down the railroad embankment that marked the city limits of Deerhaven—population 1,700.

The runner thought only briefly of the driver who had seen them. He hoped the woman wouldn't call the police, but what would she tell them? That she had seen two lovers racing madly through the streets of small town America? If she told it all, she wouldn't be believed.

His mind was too full of other things, however, to worry much about what had been seen or hadn't. The pain in his chest had grown worse and he had to concentrate all his energy on picking up his feet and putting them down again. Then they were across the tracks, headed into the open fields beyond, and he knew that the one he chased had finally made a mistake.

It was late autumn in the Ozark Mountains and the hilly fields were overgrown with sulphur weed and Johnson grass, and with the thick tangles of blackberry briars. The heavy growth would slow her down, while he, being much bigger, could bull his way through more easily. It was a bad mistake she'd made, and he began to close the gap between them.

To her credit, she did not try to zigzag. She was smart enough to know that it would only provide him with angles by which to cut her off. She just tucked her head down and ran straight on, straight and fast and hard, though he heard a rough edge to her breathing that had not been there before.

He steadily closed the gap.

The rhythm of their feet tearing through the grass was a constant whisper. The straining of their muscles was silent. Only their breathing was loud. The rain was fading away, and the moon, which had been out earlier, began to peek from the clouds once more. It seemed an uncaring witness.

The night just waited for the end.

He closed the gap. Ten feet, five feet behind her, a body length. He could almost hear her heart pounding now, and he gathered himself for the spring that would carry him onto her back and bring her down. He moved up beside her, matching her speed, but when he would have leaped, she dodged to the left and his strike missed. He skidded on wet grass, his heavy body unable to change direction as rapidly as hers, and she widened the distance between them again before he caught his balance and drove on after her.

She began to zigzag *now*, hoping he would slip and fall, but his balance remained good and he had gotten his second wind. She abandoned her new strategy after only a moment and headed for the stream that rilled along the northern border of the field. A barb wire fence kept the cattle away from the steep drop off of the creek bank. She went under the lowest strand of wire with ease, going to her belly and back to her feet in one fluid motion. He skidded behind her and went under the wire too, but he wasn't low enough to avoid the cruel barbs that raked furrows along his spine. This, too, was a mistake for her. He had not really been angry until then, not really in a rage. Now he was.

He came out from under the barbs and leaped from the high bank while she was just starting up the opposite slope of the streambed. She had not realized how much the slight grade would slow her down in her exhausted state—her legs must have felt like straw by then—and even her strong will could not make her move fast enough to avoid his attack. His shoulder struck her in the side and bowled her over, rolling her down into the welling stream below.

He came down after her, but she was already back on her feet and ready to face him. Now there was nowhere to run. She stood her ground, a wordless snarl twisting what were to him the world's most beautiful features. He matched her snarl with one of his own, though he suddenly found that he did not want to fight her. All of his anger was gone, lost in her eyes.

Perhaps she sensed his hesitation, and she came for him like a stooping hawk. Once more he used his weight as a weapon, knocking her back and down. She came up again and tried desperately to sink white teeth into his shoulder, but he had the advantage of high ground now and he knocked her down a third time. This time she rose more slowly, her eyes wide and watching. He looked into her face for any flicker of fear, or of anything else. All he saw was defiance.

He stepped back. He really did not want to fight her now. She had run well but he had caught her. Surely she could see that. And it was not as if she hadn't invited it, strutting around him as she had. He whimpered, a wet and raw sound in his throat, a request that he knew she wouldn't deny.

She didn't. He could see when the tension went out of her muscles and the fire left her eyes. She watched him for a moment longer, then dropped her gaze. She answered his whimper with one of her own.

He moved up beside her, her small head barely coming to the level of his shoulder, and a wave of tenderness washed over him. She was his now. The run was over.

He glanced up at the sound of rattling brush and saw the shadows with red eyes that had come from nowhere to rim the creek. He bristled, rumbling protectively in his throat, but it was mere instinct. No one would interfere now. The circuit had to be completed.

The female butted her nose into his chest and licked at the fur that creased his neck. He turned back toward her, ignoring the watchers above, and closed his teeth very gently on her muzzle. In a few minutes they were coupling on the soft bank of the stream. The moonlight shone down on their entwined limbs, on the faces and the muzzles, on the fur and the skin. Sometimes it shone on parts that were human; sometimes not. After a while, a chorus of howls filled the night silence.

Later, they tracked down the human driver who had seen

the frenzied insanity of the mating run, and they ripped her up like so much confetti. After all, the clan was new to the Ozark Mountains and to the small town of Deerhaven that was gripped in the isolation of its woods. None of them wanted talk of werewolves to get out, especially not now that they had begun to reproduce. They didn't want to scare away the meat they would soon be needing to feed the young.

LICENSE TO BLEED

His gold-plated Beretta is a
sweet lie.
That isn't what he uses to kill.
And why do you think the bowtie
is red?
And the shirts so easily laundered?
If it isn't that they are hard
to stain?
Have you ever seen him mussed?
Or his hair wet from a shower?
Did he ever walk into a room
without every head turning?
Maybe I should warn you that he
cannot sweat.
That he doesn't own a crucifix
or a mirror.
But it's part of his charm that
no one believes,
until too late.
His manner may be champagne.
But you gotta know his bite
is whiskey.

I AM HERE

Once there was a castle built into a mountain, and its shape was like an iron-stained skull. In it lived a beautiful but lonely woman. There were two windows, set high on the castle walls where the sockets of the massive skull would be. There was one doorway—the mouth—but the granite teeth were closed and locked and try as she might she could never break through them.

The woman stood sometimes at the stone mouth and studied the light through the cracks between the sculpted teeth. She felt the warm breeze blowing in to stir her hair and cut the chill of the room. She wanted that warmth. But there was no escape. And she was alone all through the days and nights.

She spent the long days wandering quietly through the white corridors of her castle prison. Often, she lingered at the windows and looked out at the sunshine lands so far below. In the distance ran a river and beside it nestled a tiny village. Sometimes she saw the indistinct shapes of people moving there, and she knew they went about the business of living— eating, drinking, perhaps, in the evening, making love while the cook-fires burned low.

In the castle it was forever cold, as if it were always turning winter there. The woman shivered often and there was little to cover herself with except the beautiful silk gowns that she wore. Sometimes she prayed for warmth.

Each day, at morning and evening, the woman went to a small room in the center of the castle. Always in that place she would discover a table laden with rich and exotic foods, and with water and wine to drink. On rare days she might even find a sweet and biting liquor that she relished for the silence it brought to her thoughts. Many times she tried waiting within that room to see where the feast came from. But eventually she would have to leave to take care of her body's needs, or she would fall asleep. And when she returned, or awoke, her nourishment was there.

The woman ate, though she seldom felt hungry. She drank to keep the blood flowing in her veins, though she often wondered why. Many times she cried at the table, with the tears falling away into silence. It never seemed as if anyone heard.

Each day when she went to eat, she found a wooden plate set for her to use. And each day when she left the room she took the plate with her and sat in the high windows carving words on it with a small knife. She didn't write "help" or "please." She wrote only: "I am here."

After she finished her carving, she would sail the plate out the window, watching it glide the long way toward the foot of the mountain, toward the distant village. She never saw a plate reach that far, but she kept throwing them. Day after day. Hoping. For what, she wasn't quite sure.

One night the woman sat long in the socket window of the castle. She lay on the smooth stone, looking off at the lights of the village, hearing the tiny sounds of music. She thought of people dancing together, and of lovers old and new kissing in the shadows. The longing came upon her like a fever. She pounded her fists against unyielding stone; she screamed. Her mouth seemed to tear with the sorrow and at last she rose to stand on the edge of the stone socket. The hem of her gown played around her ankles and she knew that one step would end her misery. One step and she would fall and fall.

A sound brought her pause, a shattering noise that reverberated through the entire castle. She turned from the abyss, drawing her gown close against a sudden chill. Her eyes were wide, and a little frightened. But she had to see what had made the sound, had to know if anything had, or could, change for her.

She lit a candle and forced herself out into the corridor to follow the long, winding white staircase toward the bottom floor.

She stopped on the staircase's last step, her nose telling her that something *had* changed. She smelled an odor like sweat and smoke. Not unpleasant. But new in this place. Then she saw a shadow different from any that had been here before. It was large, flickering in the glow of her candle.

Unable to resist the questions raised by that shadow, the woman went down the last step and lifted her light. She gasped. A man stood there in armor, wearing a bronze sword over his back and carrying a huge club of iron and wood. But even as she watched, the man dropped the club and reached to remove his helmet. He tossed the helm aside, and she saw that he was young and handsome, with the hair hanging to his shoulders and his eyes glowing with reflected flame.

Very slowly then, the man walked toward her, no threat in his face or in the way that he moved. And when he stopped in front of her, his eyes were warm.

The woman spoke: "Did you come to take me to the village? Can we leave this place?"

The man said nothing for a moment, only stepped to one side so she could see the mouth of the skull castle, and see that the teeth he'd broken with his club were all healed again and the door closed. A magical light played across that doorway and she knew it was locked with both of them inside.

The man took the woman's hand and went down to one knee. He kissed her fingers. Then her palm. And her wrist. It seemed clear that he had found her plates with the message scrawled across them.

The man stood and offered the woman his arm. And when she took it, he smiled and spoke for the first time:

"I am here too," he said. "Forever with you."

The woman nodded and returned his smile.

The man led her up the white stairs then. He took her to the room where her feasts were laid, to the place from which she had gathered the wooden plates that called him to her. He poured her wine and they banqueted together, first on food and then upon each other.

It did not occur to the woman to wonder how the man knew the castle so well.

COLD WHERE
YOUR LOVE LIES

It was a long walk from the city to where he could stand looking up at the small cemetery floating overhead. He'd come through the chill afternoon to get here, toiling up the long slope of Mourning Mountain to the flat table of rock where he now stood. No one else was here, but then it wasn't a place anyone visited very often. The crypts made too harsh a contrast against the purple-blue sky and the brilliant flush of the clouds. Tombs didn't match open spaces and fresh mountain winds. But he had reasons for coming here.

He set down the heavy black case he was carrying and lowered a backpack from his shoulders, letting the latter hit the ground with a thud and clank. He opened the pack and pulled out the nylon bag that held his battered tent. A smaller bag contained the structure's metal supports and anchor spikes.

In fifteen minutes he had pitched the tent and had crawled inside with his sleeping bag and the tiny foam pillow he always took camping. He closed the flaps against the cutting breeze, but left the rain cover off so he could look up through the mesh ceiling and watch the dead place drifting quietly above.

There were only two other things in his backpack, a water bottle and a harmonica. Though there wasn't any food and it had been a while since he'd eaten, he didn't feel hungry. He sipped his water, then played a lorn tune on the harmonica. It wasn't a very good tune but no one was around who could complain.

Evening passed. Night fell.

The clouds began to dissipate, and at this high altitude and this late in the winter the darkness brought an intense cold. The stars came out, but the familiar constellations were occulted by the crypts. He hadn't come to view the stars anyway.

At midnight the first pattering sounds came, interspersed with the thumps of objects striking the nylon skin of the tent. The moon was up and he went outside. Flower fall had begun. He caught a violet, a lily, a thorned rose. He caught irises and tulips and daisies. Their petals were frozen, their stems coated with ice from the high cirrostratus clouds where they'd been lying. He began to collect them into piles, separating the violets for a personal bouquet.

The fall continued for half an hour before fading away. He completed his gathering of blooms and then sat cross-legged in front of his tent, pulling his sleeping bag around his shoulders against the cold. Amid a surreal architecture built from flowers, he waited.

It wasn't long before something wet touched his bare neck. Tiny suspended droplets of fog wrapped around him, slid over his face to roil in the backwash of breath spilling from his nostrils. Within that mist, the cemetery began to drift lower and lower, until it settled atop the mountain.

He rose then, and began to walk among the crypts, letting his hands brush wet, slick marble or the roughness of granite, letting his fingers explore engravings of crosses and angels. He translated the names as if they were Braille, but his touch lingered most on phrases like "Beloved Mother," "Beloved Husband," "Beloved Son or Daughter." When he found the one he wanted, it read, "Beloved Wife."

This was the main reason he'd come.

He knelt on the wet earth in front of this crypt. A concrete urn stood empty beneath his wife's inscription and he placed the violets he'd saved within it. They were her favorite. He leaned forward, let his head rest against the cool marble of the tomb. He told his wife then, how much he loved her, how much he missed her, how much he remembered their moments together.

He did not know how much time had passed when he raised his head again, but he could tell that the fog had already begun to thin. Quickly, he worked to fill the urns on all the other crypts with the flowers he'd gathered, and despite the cold he was sheened with sweat when he was done.

Finally, he went to the black case he'd brought with him and opened it. Inside nestled twenty-five objects for the twenty-five crypts. Each crypt had a wide slot in its door and he fed an object through each of those slots. Then he stepped back and stood watching.

The last of the fog began to lift, and with it rose the crypts. As his wife's tomb began to drift skyward, he raised a hand and waved. And through the glass window of the crypt, his wife waved back. She waved with one hand while the other held the object he'd given her up to her mouth. Blood from that gift coated her lips and chin.

She was smiling. He smiled back.

Such an enlightened world, he thought. Even vampires were not to be killed, only imprisoned for human safety and set floating in a pleasant place. Most people had forgotten this cemetery was ever here; fewer still came to visit. Today's humanity had little use for ceremony. But not everyone had lost track of the old sentiments, the old celebrations. *He* had not. Nor had his wife. She'd always loved Valentine's Day. And he never failed to remember her favorite day by giving her a heart.

SONG TO A ROSE

Do you guide the blade
that savages the petal
for love stained mouths,
that swallows sin like pomegranates,
like the lips that feed the throat
on war,
like the sex that burns the prophet,
that rakes the leaves of despair,
that silvers the hair of once dark beauty?
Does your hand wave the flag
that pierces the rise of joy?
Does your hand weave the cloth
that covers the shame of spring?
Are you the one who makes his god,
who freezes the heart of gold into lead
and pours it upon the eye of winter,
which looks upon a hated surrender,
which saves the blood the color of...
Rose?

THIEF OF EYES

She had the lips that Satan dreamed of in his long fall to hell. That's why I followed her down that nameless, narrow alley in "the city care forgot."

I'd been riding all day, coming up out of Texas on my painted whore of a Harley, and an impulse sent me angling off the Vieux Carre exit and into the French Quarter. I'd been to New Orleans many times and never found anything there I couldn't live without, but my life had been governed by whims of late and I saw no reason to stop paying attention to them now.

It was cool but not cold in the mid-October Southern night. A rain had come and gone and I'd caught just the sprinkle at the tail end of it. The crowds of tourists and locals on Bourbon and Royal streets had barely paused in their ceaseless mingling, and the sheer carnival weight of people and their forced gaiety was too much for me even riding past.

I took a street whose name I didn't catch, thinking I'd head down to Esplanade and follow it along to the quiet of City Park. Then the girl in the silver dress came walking along and smiled at me when I slowed to stare. An instant later she swayed down an alley and I lost sight of her. But I had to see those lips again, and the hair that fell halfway down her back in a soft explosion of brunette curls.

Two good things about motorcycles. They turn like dreams and you can always find a parking space. Wheeling around, I backed the bike into a narrow gap between a mule-drawn carriage and a neon blue Geo. Then I kicked down the silver talon side stand and unsaddled.

There was nothing in the saddlebags but some clothes that weren't worth stealing and the goggles I wore on the highway. Neither Texas nor Louisiana had a helmet law. I locked the bike and it was only a few steps to the alley where the girl had disappeared. I didn't hesitate.

My boots clicked on dusky smooth paving stones, and buildings of reddish brick lifted on either side. A dozen yards down the alley stood a black, wrought-iron gate worked in the style of a French Quarter balcony. But beyond the gate there opened a plaza whose architecture was different than anything I'd ever seen in the Quarter.

I'd always thought the Quarter ran Spanish and French in taste, but this place looked...Central American jungle temple-ish. Red brick had given way to walls of smooth gray stone that seemed to lean forward in a gentle curve over the plaza. It had gotten too dark to make out clearly the frescoed figures that adorned those walls. Besides, I was more interested in the door that stood open across from me. Above it gleamed a dim sign—Chac Mool—and through it I caught a glimpse of silver silk on swaying hips.

Brushing a few rosary beads of rain from my leather jacket, I drifted unnoticed into the club. For that was certainly what this place was. Smoke fogged the interior, which was set up like a temple to the kind of gods my Catholic upbringing had never prepared me to worship. The floor was all stone flaggings, placed without mortar. Soot-dark statues stood in what seemed a thousand corners. The people in charge of atmosphere here were doing their job well. Even the hand-worked stone foliage on the walls reeked of jungles.

Making my way through a low, throbbing music that beat in my chest like a tripartite heart, I watched for any flash of silver amid the scattered and hazy purple light that rose from a hundred sources in the walls and carvings. To one side was a massive bar with ranked rows of cut glass bottles rising behind it; to the other was a dance floor where half a dozen couples linked their bodies in rhythm to the slow, harmonic pulse in the air.

I stopped between two stoneware barrels in which were rooted small trees, their leaves redolent of cigarette smoke and whisky, but also of something else, something like monkeys and jade and sacrifices. From here I could watch the dance floor and wait for the silver woman. Something told me to expect her there.

Against a sculpted stone column nearby leaned a lip-pierced girl with dread-locked hair of nail-polish red. She wore a short black skirt over a crimson leotard, with black, lace-up work boots and the new-age stoner smile of someone who'd sipped too much ginkgo and ginseng. Amid the shadows and flickering light she seemed to writhe against the column, and the column seemed to writhe back.

I shook my head, trying to clear the vision, and the mist around me flashed electric blue as strobes bit at the smoke. A new music began. Wild. Hallucinogenic. The music of fakirs and dreaming mystics. I was given to ZZ Top and Black Sabbath myself, but I recognized the wail of sitars when I heard them. Hypnotic they were, as wicked as silk on sweat.

They brought the woman I wanted.

I watched her take the dance floor in a feral flash of limbs. And she moved like an exquisite machine, all gleaming and supple and dangerous. Her gaze bruised across mine as she spun, and I saw her eyes as gray as pearled ashes.

Those eyes. Her dance. They reminded me of words that had come to me one morning as I hammered down the freeway at a 100 plus on my bike:

"Death is a pale-eyed harlequin, lovely as the earliest slice of dawn."

In those days I'd been a poet, but that meant nothing now.

I took off my jacket and draped it over an unoccupied chair, then walked out on the dance floor in faded jeans, T-shirt and boots. I know what I look like, with the silver axe earring, the long hair and beard, the tattoos that ink their way from elbows to wrists. I look like a hardcore biker and it was an image I'd cultivated. But inside I was just another scared, sick man.

I didn't ask the woman to dance—she was doing quite well by herself—but just watched with one shoulder braced against a knuckle-worn railing behind which bands could play. A waitress with short, spiked hair of white and contact lenses that made her eyes into yellow smiley faces handed me a beer. I hadn't asked for it but it was the kind I usually drank—Negra Modelo. When I went to pay her she shook her head. Her lips curved with a smile that seemed to drip shadows, and her gaze flicked toward the dancer and away. I understood.

"Gil, you're not in Texas anymore," I whispered to myself as the waitress stalked off. The beer tasted as coldly bitter and delicious as ever. Better, since I scarcely drank at all anymore.

The sitars moaned to a halt and the woman in silver stopped dancing and turned toward me. She took the Modelo from my hand and drank, her dark hair falling back over her shoulders as she tilted her head up and her throat worked. An unpleasant flutter roiled in my stomach, though I tried not to show it. All across the woman's neck was a purple-haze webbing of ugly bruises that were just starting to bleach toward yellow.

The woman lowered the bottle from her perfect lips and handed it back. Her smile seemed to know what I was thinking, what I was wondering. Who had hurt her? Was she bruised in other ways? Or could she have done this to herself? Was she crazy?

She leaned toward me, her hand reaching to rest against my T-shirt, just under the heart. Through the thin cotton I felt the coolness of her fingers where they were damp from the sweat of the bottle.

Other music played now, but I heard her words clearly through its white noise: "The past is a dead soul. There is no moment other than this. And in this moment I am Lyla and I am what you want."

She turned and walked away from me then, stopping just long enough to scoop up my jacket and slide the worn leather on over her silk dress. I left the beer on the table and followed; the jacket had cost me 200 bucks.

Heels clicking, Lyla started up a staircase I hadn't noticed before. It spiraled upward in wrought iron and I put my hand on the rail to follow, then quickly jerked that hand back. The iron felt moist and warm, almost...alive. I wanted to think it was just condensation on the metal caused by long accumulations of smoke and the touch of greasy hands, but I couldn't quite make myself grab the rail again as I went up behind the woman.

At the top of the stairs, Lyla turned left, her skirt swishing electrically across her thighs as her stocking-less legs scissored. I held back a moment, as some sound prickled cold at my scalp. To my right was a hall carpeted in moss-deep green, with a mahogany balustrade to one side that was intricately worked with carvings of eagles, snakes, and demigods. On the other side of the hall stood a row of doors from behind which came faint moans and gasps that could have been sex or death. Or both.

Not really wanting to hear more, I turned quickly after Lyla then. At the end of the hall she'd opened a pair of narrow doors filled with smoked and beveled glass, and as she saw me coming she stepped through them onto a balcony. I joined her, moved to lean over the black rail beside her.

"That's my jacket," I said inanely.

She chuckled, the sound low and full of a sandpaper rasp that made my mouth go dry. Her face turned toward me; her eyes shivered my spine. She smelled of absinthe and tigers.

"Death is a pale-eyed harlequin," she said, "lovely as the earliest slice of dawn. And he is a fiend, a razor, a rotted angel. He wears the silk of sins within his cloak of bones."

I jolted with the shock of hearing my private thoughts tossed back to me with embellishments.

"How—?" I started to ask, but she stopped me with the knuckle of her index finger pressed coolly against my lips.

"The parade," she whispered.

And there was a parade—though I had not seen it forming,

had not heard it coming. Below in the street, where the pavement glistened in wet black, people were passing with measured tread. Each of them carried a torch on a bamboo pole; flambeaux they were called here.

I'd been to parades in New Orleans before. They are not quiet. But this one was. The marchers held their pace steady, their faces hidden by the brims of feathered hats beneath the licking shadows cast by the torches. Not even their boots rang on the cement. In that silence I held my breath, waiting for something that I knew I didn't want to happen.

Above us, the skies began slowly to clear and the moon flashed fragments of its face through torn folds of what looked like draped, gray fabric. At that moment all the marchers lowered their torches and glanced up. At us. Or at Lyla. And all of them wore parrot-feathered masks through which curving crimson horns protruded where the eyes should have been.

I gripped the balcony railing tight, my fingers clenched and bloodless. My lungs sucked in a breath that tasted raw in my throat. As if a wind had shifted to drive the sound, I heard again the shuddering moans from the hallway beyond the glass doors. It felt to me as if something like an animal-god stalked there, as if I could turn and see a thing of scorpions and antlers and red-bruised eyes crouched at my shoulder.

I did not turn. I would not turn. Though the thing wanted me to.

Lyla touched me on the shoulder.

I jumped, glanced at her with widened eyes, expecting to see that she wasn't quite human. But she was only herself, slender, lovely, fragile as a spell of cool weather in a tropical summer. The sounds from the corridor behind me subsided; the parade moved away down the street.

Silly, I told myself. I was letting my imagination run without a bit in its mouth. I forced myself to breathe again, tried to convince myself that I was too much of a "bad-ass" to run from sounds and masks. The convincing worked. Though it was a near thing. I managed to back my nervous system down from near panic mode to mere alert status.

Lyla seemed not to have felt anything strange. "Why did you follow me here?" she asked.

Such a question, from another woman at another time, might have been a cue for me to say something charming and roguish and appropriately poetic. But I couldn't wrap my thoughts around anything that didn't sound either afraid or fossilized. Instead, I told her the truth. As I knew it.

"I've been looking for something. Or someone. I thought it might be you."

She leaned back against the filigreed ironwork of the rail. The jacket slid open, showing her body beneath, enhanced rather than hidden by the supple tautness of her dress. Her nipples thrust against the silk. At the fulcrum of her thighs I saw the shadowy press of her pubic bone against tissue thin cloth. My own body, already wired tight, responded instantly.

Lyla reached a decision then. She shook her head, her eyes hollow within the dark violin of the night. "Not looking for," she said. "Running from." And she said it with such absolute conviction that I didn't argue. I couldn't.

"Death hunts you," she added. "Is it the lover? The rotted angel? The pale-eyed harlequin? What's killing you?"

I should have been surprised by her question. I wasn't.

"How did you know?" I asked.

She smiled, her mouth a battle line of shadows and light. Then she looked away, dropped one hand to her belly to let her burgundy nails swirl against the silver silk.

"You saw the name of this place," she replied, a cryptic response if I'd ever heard one.

"Yes. Something Mule?" I knew the true name was much more exotic but didn't quite recall what the sign outside had read. What difference did it make anyway?

But in some way it made a difference to Lyla. She laughed, with such genuine humor that my anxieties of moments ago faded almost completely.

"What?" I asked, grinning.

She was still laughing as she looked back at me. "It's called Chac Mool," she finally managed. And then, without laughter: "Only certain people come to this place."

I frowned. "Why?"

"It means...," she started. And paused. The moment lingered before she rewrote her script and asked me a question instead.

"Do you believe some people have a greater sense of their mortality than others?"

I didn't have to think to answer that one. I'd written poems about it in the long ago.

"Yeah," I said.

Lyla nodded. "You and I are among that number. And every customer in this bar."

Again there was a silence, before I began: "We awoke from scarred dreams...."

Lyla finished: "...carrying death's bruises all the way to the bone."

I wondered if she'd read that poem, published almost a decade past in a magazine long since gone, or if the ending to the line I'd written then had been obvious to her now because of who she was and how she felt.

I told her something only my doctors knew.

"Back a few years ago I had a motorcycle wreck. In Mexico. Got a blood transfusion. Something wasn't clean. The needles. Or maybe the blood itself."

"And this year you stopped taking your meds," she said.

"Yes."

"So did I. Ten years ago."

"You have it, too?" I asked.

"Something worse."

I didn't ask her what. I really didn't care. If she had the bubonic plague, it wouldn't matter. Any sickness that kills you is only going to kill you once.

Instead I said. "Ten years is a long time to live with...whatever it is."

It had begun to rain again, the sound spattering off the city, the wetness of it misting across where we stood.

"Not long enough," Lyla said. "Even though you learn so intimately of sacrifice, ten years is not quite long enough."

She took my hand to lead me from the balcony.

Some part of me that wasn't completely under Lyla's spell wanted to say: "Just give me my jacket and let me get out of here." But that part was far too small to listen to. I held Lyla's hand instead and followed her back through the glass doors and down the carpeted hall. There were no sounds now, either from the bar below or from the rooms which we passed.

All the doors looked the same; none of them had numbers on them. But Lyla had no trouble finding one that fronted an empty room. She led me through into a place of candles where the bed had been piled high with furs and silks. The candles were tallow, alabaster-pale with crimson wicks, and arrayed in an intricate mandala around the bed.

Lyla released my hand, stepped over the candles and turned to face me within a cone of light that painted her face innocent. She took off my jacket and tossed it to me.

"Go if you want," she said. For an instant it seemed as if her eyes wanted me to go. But her body was too full of curves and promise. She had to know I wouldn't leave her now.

I threw the jacket aside with a growl and stepped over the threshold of the candles to join her. She came into my arms instantly, her hunger apparent in the pillow-soft flush of her lips as they opened under mine.

I kissed her hard enough to bruise, let my tongue stab against hers and swirl around it in a war of want. Lyla's hands dropped to my waist, tugged at my belt, at the snaps of my jeans. She broke the kiss, drew back to lock her gaze to mine.

"They dream in heat," she murmured. "Of eyes and those who suffer for their sins."

It sounded like a verse I might have written years ago, though I couldn't remember the line and didn't care anyway.

"Fuck poetry," I snapped.

Lyla's irises were meres of storm-gray water. She dragged me down on top of her on the bed, pulled my mouth to the hollow of her throat. I tasted her skin, like taffy, felt the wing-beat of her pulse through my lips. Her hands slid over me, working at my shirt, at my jeans. My own hands found the hem of her silver dress and slipped it above her satin thighs to her waist. She wore nothing underneath.

Lyla's fingernails scraped wickedly across the small of my back and she clutched my buttocks, urging me forward until my body slid against hers and we linked. Without thought now, I thrust against her. She matched me, her arms viseing around my neck, her legs forming an arch through which I took her.

A scalpel of pain stabbed my shoulder as Lyla nuzzled and bit. But I only growled, my hands tangled in her hair, her hands tangled in mine. The bed rattled beneath us; silks and furs were kicked to the floor to smolder unnoticed against candles.

The light wavered in the room, sending shadows scattering over the walls and floor. And Lyla and I fought each other in the rasp of friction, muscles straining like cables tested to their limits. Sweat ran—on my face, down my back under Lyla's sharp touch. Our breaths came in punctuated gasps.

She reached for my hand, pulled it from her hair and pushed it down. Her chin lifted; she offered me her throat. I didn't understand until she herself pressed my fingers against her neck. I choked out a strangled, "no," but my thumb shifted, my hand tightened.

My other hand joined the first.

I heard Lyla moan then, my own moan following. From all around in the room came echoes. I heard the beat of hearts that seemed more ancient than mine, and whimpers of pleasure that hardly sounded human. There was too much sound, too much movement. But my mind noted those things only in passing. Nothing mattered but the woman I lay with, her beautiful face twisted in need as she closed her eyes and began to pump her body desperately against mine.

My hips began to lose the rhythm, began to flail as Lyla

thrashed beneath me. I bit at my lower lip, trying to prolong the moment, and at the very edge of my release Lyla opened her eyes again and gazed up at me. Her irises were no longer an ashen gray. They flamed as bright as quicksilver mirrors, a brightness that filled even her pupils.

In those mirrors I saw a reflection. Mine. And others! Over my shoulder swirled a nimbus of light clouded with shadow, filled with interlaced serpents and altars of lichened stone, filled with priests wearing crowns of parrot feathers, holding high obsidian knives that writhed with blood from bodies straining toward death.

And there were worse things there. One worse thing!

I shouted, tried to tear myself away from the impossible reality that I saw in Lyla's eyes. But my hands could not loose themselves from around her throat, as if she had teeth there. And with the bite of those bruises and the ligatures of her limbs, Lyla bound me. Clinging. Clinging. Her face was wild; her hips thrust and thrust. She came, and it burned like acid, but the pain of it milked my own release and I emptied myself inside of her.

As if my body's betrayal of itself was a signal, jade-clawed hands grasped my head from above and tore me from Lyla's embrace. I struggled, grabbing at wrists on which the skin was slick and putrid. I smelled musk and wet fur and rot; my ears filled with a static of tiny crackles and droning murmurs, like demon voices whispering with rain. I think I screamed. But I was held as easily as a toy.

"Lover," the thing that held me hissed near my ear.

But the word wasn't directed at me. And it was Lyla who responded, rising to her knees on the bed, her head lowered, her shoulders shaking.

"Loverrr!" the being repeated.

Lyla looked up. Her face was veiled with tears but the flesh beneath seemed...molten and fluid. I stopped struggling.

The candles guttered and went out. But the shadows they'd thrown were still there, alive in the room as they flapped like umbral wings about Lyla's form. Lyla moved toward me on her knees then, the shadows extending from her, curving around to connect and flow into the shape of whatever being held me so still. The two of them were one. Almost.

"Yes," the being said. "Let us pray."

Lyla shivered, but her hands lifted. She reached for my face, her fingers caressing over my mouth, spidering up my cheeks. I tried to pull my head away but had no strength to fight my captor.

"In jungle temples," Lyla said, as if speaking ritual, "they took hearts and ate them smoking with blood on their altars. They took eyes to see through other minds. Their sacrifices lived forever."

Lyla's face caved into a ghastly rictus. Her whole body seemed to come unformed, to shimmer like a negative of the shadows that were still woven around her. But her fingers felt intensely real as they touched at the dark circles beneath my sockets and begin to press.

Then I did struggle, with eyes closing. And I know I screamed. But the woman's touch was iron and did not waver as I tore futilely at her wrists to pull her hands down and away.

And still her voice came...shouting now, over mine.

"They are the gods of rain and jaguars. Who did not die when their people died. Who moved with the Mayans and the Aztecs and the Spanish. Who take through me their sacrifices of souls and seed. And let me live."

A light burst in my head, filled with bolts of color and bright pointillistic shapes, and the darkness that followed with the tearing of flesh was more total than any night should be.

I stopped screaming.

* * * * * * *

"The parade," Lyla whispered. "Begin the parade."

In a dress of silver silk she stood on her balcony, beside her a presence, an inchoate something that swirled like a storm, giving off tendrils of darkness that stabbed her in a hundred places but left no wounds. Perhaps that thing of jade claws and hornet voice had once been a god in the Central American jungles. But now it festered and preyed and lived like a parasite in a midnight temple bar in the concrete swamp of New Orleans.

I saw it. I saw through it. For it wore my eyes among others in a face of clots and pus and rot.

And beneath us, in step beneath the flicker of torches, the marchers came. A hundred of them. A thousand perhaps. The last in line wore a leather jacket but moved like all the others, one foot in front of another as his parade...passed.

PORTRAIT OF
HER IN DARKNESS

Eyes,
yellow emptiness, circular scars
smoke screens for the soulless

Hair,
fair as night, sweet as shadows
perfumed with the odor of decay

Skin,
white of bones, a chalk beauty
the tincture of pearled eggs

Body,
adored by glances, sculpted sin
all thoughts abandoned to lust

LIKE A BROKEN GOD

like
a
broken
god
he
drifts
in
hunger

VOODOO GODS

Her body spooned against me,
with whiskey breath.
I watch her wasted,
hear her tears drip sick on my pillow.
I want her touch; I won't get it.
She's too caught in scarlet prayers
to voodoo gods
she claims not to believe in.
But I know she *does* believe.
She worships with
despair and alcohol,
feels pain to know she lives.
And I wonder how long it'll be
before she converts me
to her faith.

FED ON NIGHT

fed
on
night
her
heart
grows
bold

HUNTER'S MOON

Leroy Dyson stood against the wall of the observation deck and studied the men and women of his seven person crew. *Six person crew*, he corrected himself. There were only six other crewmembers now on Moon Base Freedom, although over the next few years many more ships were scheduled to arrive with their cargos of settlers and supplies.

Artificial light always made the observation deck feel sterile to Dyson, and normally the emergency meteor shields covering the windows here would be lowered out of the way to reveal the black sky and bright stars. No one at Freedom base was afraid of the sight of space. But Dyson had closed the shields now. Considering what was happening and why he'd called this meeting, he *needed* them closed.

"All right. Let's get started," he said.

The hubbub of voices and the random milling about of confused people subsided. Gazes began to turn to meet Dyson's. An absence was noted.

"Where's Samuels?" a crewman named Mark Howard called.

"That's why I wanted this meeting," Dyson said. He paused, cleared his throat, and: "Samuels is dead."

Now he had everyone's *full* attention.

"But I just..." Heather Tate started, bit her lip, and stopped.

"How did it happen?" Ed Carmichael asked in a hushed voice.

Dyson looked around the room. Half an hour ago there had been a body here. And blood. He and his second-in-command, Lana Jackson, had cleaned up the mess.

There'd been a lot of mess.

Dyson glanced at Jackson. She'd changed out of her stained clothes. As had he. Now, she offered him a reassuring smile. He gave a slight nod before looking back at the others.

"Samuels was murdered," Dyson said finally. "I discovered the body a little while ago right here on the observation deck."

The general hubbub returned, twice as loud for having been gone. *Some* voices were even louder.

"Oh my God!" Heather Tate blurted.

"Who?" Mark Howard demanded. "Who did it?"

Then everyone realized that, since the entire crew except for the murder victim was here, the murderer had to be here too. Silence came rampaging in. Pupils dilated. Eyes darted left and right, trying to look everywhere at once. Gazes locked, then fled from each other. People put distance between themselves and the next person over. Fear had taken hold. Terror began to build.

"You already know it had to be one of us," Dyson said, his voice firm enough to cut through the incipient hysteria. For a brief moment, a kind of calm returned.

Dyson glanced again at Lana. Her face was strange and he knew she was remembering the body parts and the tattered viscera, and the low gravity roll of smelly copper-red droplets across the observation deck's floor. Samuels had not died easily.

"How long had he been dead when you found him?" Mark Howard asked.

"Not long at all."

"It could have been any one of us," Jessica Rollins cried. "None of us were together. The base is so big. So many places to hide. So—"

"A big question is why?" Howard interrupted. "*Why* was Samuels killed?"

"I suspect he surprised someone doing something they didn't want anyone else to know about," Dyson said.

"Like what?" Howard demanded.

"Lana and I have an idea about that," Dyson said, glancing

yet again at his second-in-command. She was looking toward the sealed windows. Her brunette curls fell across her face, but he could see the swell of her lower lip and the faint, pure glisten of the whites of her eyes.

She was so beautiful to him, and he'd been secretly sleeping with her ever since they'd left earth. His gaze shifted to her belly, and it almost seemed as if his vision could penetrate straight through her NASA-issue coveralls and into her womb. She was four months pregnant, with more than one fetus, though no one except he and she knew it yet. He could not help but smile to himself when he thought of how their babies would be the first earth children to be born off planet.

"What kind of idea?" Heather Tate whined. "And what are you going to do to protect us from this murderer?"

Dyson blinked, brought his thoughts back to the problem at hand. His gaze found Heather. And the others. He sighed.

"Nothing," he said.

For a long moment there was silence, and confusion. Dyson took an instant to press the switch that opened the shielding over the windows. The steel covers began to sink toward the floor. Star shine flooded in through the thick glass. Then came a brighter light. Moon light. A streaming silver fire poured in to bathe them all in ghostly luminescence.

Dyson moved toward Lana, imagining their offspring being born under the glow of this new world. *Their* new world.

Theirs alone.

Lana's form shuddered; she began to change. She'd always been able to control it, until the hormonal surges induced by her pregnancy.

The crew's silence dissolved; they began to scream. Dyson didn't care. His thoughts were on other things. A steady supply of live food would be coming for Lana and the children on other ships over the next months. And by the time earth wised up and new food and supplies stopped arriving, Dyson would have the water synthesis program operational and the hydroponics gardens fully established. There would be enough small animals of several species to provide breeding populations, and the gardens would be able to feed a carefully selected and maintained herd of *larger animals* for use as…meat.

Dyson's mouth cracked wide in a smile. He let himself go. His spine began to curve. Coarse hair erupted all over his body. The crew's screaming grew louder but he scarcely heard it over the tearing of his flesh and the crackling of bones rearranging themselves beneath his skin. It was *time* their race had a world of its own, he thought.

The window shields clanged all the way open. Dyson and Lana began to howl in unison. And from Lana's womb came answering howls. One. Two. Three. More. The pack was in fine voice tonight, as into the room poured the savage radiance of the moon, a moon that is always full when you're living upon it.

NIGHT RAPTURES

You are standing in the empty darkness of your house. In your office, alone. Or so it seems. Only just a moment before a sound awakened you, a single booming note like a door slamming on a vacuum. There is nothing outside to account for that sound, no storm whose thunder may have cried out, no wind, no rain, not even autumn leaves tumbling down the street. It is quiet inside the house as well, quiet as the womb when both mother and infant sleep, and like in the womb you are surrounded by warmth.

You like to keep the place warm at night. Always.

Your eyes are open but you see nothing except the dim blurs of chairs, unlit lamps, bookcases against the walls, and the fine mahogany desk where you do your work. These things do not frighten you. Their shapes are familiar, comforting. There can be nothing here to frighten you at all. All is as it should be.

But then, why does your heart pump so fast? Why do your hands sweat and your ears strain to draw in a silence that seems pregnant with...possibilities?

You force silly apprehension aside and move forward, hands out to feel the way even though there is nothing here to trip you. The shadow of a lamp looms and it is this that you seek, hoping for light to dispel the nagging, prickling fear that rides a shoulder and whispers to an ear, whispers to a mind, "that sound was not natural."

It is a foolish thought, you know. It could only have been some hollow booming in your own head, a specter left from the unremembered dream that had broken just as your eyes opened. Such things occur all the time. They even have a name—hypnopompic hallucinations. You know that word, having used it in a book once. You are, after all, a writer and should know such things. But still, you will feel better when the light is on.

Your leg brushes now against the surface of the table where the lamp sits. Your hand trails lightly across the wood's surface, fingertips reading the polished grain as if it is Braille. Your eyes almost see its rich color. You have always desired fine things, ever since childhood when you lived on the streets half the time and had nothing. Now you have everything, or almost everything. Your hand touches the base of the lamp and fingers crawl up its trunk like a daddy longlegs up a tree. You touch the black knob that switches the light on. It is small and hard under your fingers, like a nipple when it's cold.

A twist of the wrist and a hot buttered glow floods the room from the soft-white, 60 watt bulb that burns behind the parchment colored lampshade. You smile. The room is just as expected. There is nothing here that you have not touched and used. You are something of a recluse since becoming famous, and have spent much time in this room. It is a second skin to you. Only, it is large enough to move around inside. Sometimes, you think of yourself as a butterfly in a square chrysalis.

You turn, still smiling, relaxing, thinking how fear is such a primitive and wasteful emotion. Then you realize that, after all, it would have been better not to have turned on the light, better not to have seen the thing that moves toward you from the direction of the bedroom, better to have let it find you in the dark.

You would like to scream now, but your mouth is all stopped up with terror and your limbs are too rigid to move as an unexpected houseguest approaches. Memories come unbidden, memories of the time since you became famous and an object of fascination and desire to millions.

You don't go out much anymore but sometimes the fans come here. They find you despite the unlisted number, the unlisted address, and they make you sick—the impassioned youths who wish they were Jack Kerouac, the little old ladies with their Cozies in their hands, thinking they can be the next Agatha Christie and wanting a pat on the head from a real writer who will tell them they have *talent*.

Worst of all are those who want to "collaborate" with you, meaning they want you to write their wonderful, amazing story and split the money with them. All of them are worthless, their skills miserable. Their adulation has locked you into your own home, but you have a honeyed revenge as you destroy their dreams by laughing at their pitiful ideas and pitifully scribbled stories. It is nearly the only source of enjoyment they have left you, and you always make the most of it.

But then had come one who was different, more lovely than the others, with green eyes and dark hair full of luster. Red lips were such a cliché but she wore them as if they weren't. Of course she wanted to be a writer. Of course she wanted *you* to help write her story, some nonsense about New Orleans voodoo. But you ignored such absurdities, invited her in, and began her seduction. It was not difficult and you thought that she must have intended it when she came. She certainly returned a kiss readily enough.

You had known many women, most of them young girls who worshipped you as "The Author," and you had used and humiliated them. But this girl with the green eyes did not seem like those others. She did not soften as you touched her, and she watched your every move until you grew uncomfortable.

And later, in the bedroom, she had laughed when you ordered her to crawl. She had laughed at your sagging belly and at the sagging thing between your legs. She'd laughed harder when you started to cry. Until your hands went around her slim throat and turned white with the strain of killing her.

It took a long time before the woman ceased struggling, and, after, you had fled the room, unable to bear any longer the touch or sight of her corpse. You had never gone back into that room, not even to bury her. You closed and locked the door, turned up the air-conditioner and burned incense to cover the smell. And you slept in your office among your books.

There had been no questions, no one who missed her or thought—at any rate—to look for her in *your* home. It was as if she had always been a blank page and even *you* had forgotten her after a while, as you have forgotten many things. But now, the door to the bedroom is no longer locked and she is coming toward you. And now she *is* crawling, though you don't think it is a sign of submission.

You stumble away from her, falling against and upsetting the lamp. It crashes to the floor but does not go out, and it casts two shadows on the ceiling where there should be only one. Then she is before you, rising to her knees and from there to her feet. Her pretty mouth is rigid in death, her lips blackened with dried blood where she had bitten almost through her tongue as you strangled her. You note somewhere in the back of your shrieking mind that the flies have been at her and that things wriggle beneath the sloughing skin that you would prefer not to see. Only her hair still seems lovely, though it has lost some of its luster, only the hair and the one green eye that does not hang from its socket.

She reaches and her hands enfold you, dragging you into her embrace. Your throat bulges around a scream as her mouth comes down and her lips thrust yours aside. Her tongue writhes into your throat, the bitten tip flopping around like a fish dying on the banks of a stream. The kiss is long and very cold, and it roars in your blood. You surge away, retching, but the wall is at your back and she only smiles. Skin tears loose from her jaws until the smile becomes permanent, and her hands are on you again, cupping your face. Her grip is strong, agonizing, paralyzing. You know that you are about to die.

The woman tugs and your spine creaks, then gives. Pain razors nerves as your head is ripped free of its shoulders and spun aloft. For an instant, you see the world swirl in mad circles, bookshelves, fallen lamp, curtains, rugs, ceiling, walls, headless torso spouting fluid.

But just when you are sure that death has come, it is denied.

Once more she kisses you, and some of whatever animates *her* slips between *your* lips like a sacramental host. She chuckles and sets your head on your desk where it sticks bloodily to the dark, sweet wood. Her dead fingers reach with crimson nails to turn on your computer. And she sits in your chair as a blank screen appears. Her rotting gaze finds yours.

"Now," she murmurs, her voice like gravel over glass. "About that collaboration."

LIKE A WHISPER

He slips among her dreams
like a whisper,
pulls her to him through her sleeping eyes.
With no mouths, yet they kiss.
They swirl in the air
like diaphanous smoke,
until with frictioned atoms grown hot
they explode upward into sky,
swirling through the wakes
of jet-liners
and night-hunting eagles.
And then the ozone
beckons.
They spiral through into blasted new light
of a sun that hemorrhages
over a fragile horizon.
With abandon and speed,
on adrenaline and dark-matter wings,
they dive into the sun's corona
like coupling angels.
Through fire they race,
through sun and planets,
loving through the rings of Saturn,
laughing at the gambols of comets,
pouting at the loneliness
of Pluto.

Outward, outward, outward,
past nebulae and novae,
past gravity wells that tear into dust
alien ships and stars,
together like rogue moons
they search for universe's end,
and don't care if they never
find it.

SHE'S A KILLER

Everywhere I look in the darkness, I see her watching me
Faded scarlet on her lips, dry chalk in her face
Eyes of need that beg into mine
A kiss so sharp it pricks like wine
Only wish I'd seen in time
She's a killer

Beneath the moonlight, her hands reach out to capture me
Ivory thorns in her hair, dark wind at her back
Open those lips and the room goes cold
What she offers? A body unsouled
All the deaths that were foretold
She's a killer

In the pearl of dawn, the dreams she gives come to life
Gleaming tears in her eyes leave fangs in my mind
Screaming to white, I await being taken
Heart twisted shut and breath so shaken
By all the memories her teeth awaken
I'm a killer

PRINCE OF
THE DARK TRAIL

Author's Note: The next two stories, "Prince of the Dark Trail" and "Unicorn Lost," are quite different from what has gone before and what comes after. No gore or violence in these. No sex. I hope you enjoy them anyway, and I'll say a little more about them and why they are in this collection in the section called "About the Stories."

Once upon a time, there lived a pale angel with owl green eyes and hair the color of a polished copper penny. She dwelt in a land of snow and shadows, a land where gorges of darkness sliced the twilight fields.

She had a great talent, did this angel. But she doubted herself. Of course, she had reasons for her doubts, but those reasons came from outside of her, not from within. Her spirit had not been tarnished.

Far to the south of the angel there lived a prince, half wicked, half good, who believed in her. He believed so hard that one day there came up a wind to carry her flying from her misty morning land to the hot and humid clime where he dwelt.

The prince met the angel with love and kisses, and took her with him to show her the kingdom that he ruled. On a long stretch of dark trail, with the sunlight spilling like golden dust through the black limbs of oaks, he offered her a share of that kingdom. History recorded her answer as "yes."

UNICORN LOST

The unicorn came out of a distant rain that spilled like threads of taffy from concrete-gray sky to sober earth. I watched him cross the purple sage toward me, with his gleaming coat and the single horn that spiraled from his forehead like an accusing finger.

It was a lonely time for me. I had just recently lost my wife to Texas and my son didn't much care for the poor. Which I was. A month before the unicorn, I'd taken to living in a tent of institutional green in a field of wild flowers in the wilderness of Wyoming. It sat just off Highway 25, and the arrival of a myth was a welcome break from counting cars and contrails.

Setting aside my can of pork 'n beans, I tidied up my immediate surroundings in honor of my approaching guest. Unfortunately, the rain had faded before it reached my tent, leaving my campsite as dusty and parched as the belly of some cast-off canteen in the forlorn heat of the desert.

That was the first thing the unicorn did for me when he arrived—give me drink. He bent his elegant neck, touched his silver-laced horn to a stone beside my tent, and a gush of fresh water broke free to rivulet the dry gray earth past my feet. I cupped my hands in the stream and lifted them to sip. The taste was good, reminding me of mist on the lower slopes of Kilimanjaro in early spring. It made me sad in a way, for I'd never visited Kilimanjaro.

"Thank you," I said, not showing my sadness.

The unicorn nodded and slowly squatted across from me,

sitting like an old, old man whose xylophone bones creak and crack in the twilight.

"I am confused," the unicorn said.

"I know the feeling," I agreed.

"Everything is so different," the unicorn continued, as if I had not spoken. "I recall when there were buffalo here like lemmings. And when feathered warriors rode variations of myself across these plains."

He gestured with his horn toward the nearby freeway where big trucks and SUV's caromed along like pinballs in a video arcade.

"I do not know why they now put stone rivers through the land where buffalo and horses and warriors no longer go."

"I know why," I said.

He looked at me curiously. "Do enlighten me, please."

"The horses fled long ago for softer duties elsewhere. The buffalo became songs and a cause and that was the death of them. The warriors lay about you in bleached skulls blanketed with fine layers of meteoric dust. They're extinct."

"That tells me why the horses and buffalo and warriors are no longer here," the unicorn said, frowning so that the sun cooled a few degrees. "But it does not explain the stone rivers, which is what I questioned you about."

"How do you think the horses traveled elsewhere?" I asked. "How do you think the people filled the museums of the world with the stuffed causes of buffalo and warriors?"

"This makes sense," the unicorn said, nodding. And then: "I believe I have heard of you before. Days ago in Texas, I spoke to a woman who seems to have known you."

"My wife?" I asked eagerly.

"A woman, at least."

"What did she tell you of me?"

"She said that you were poor and ugly."

"True," I said.

"And that you spouted many strange things. I do not believe she understood strange things."

I nodded. "My wife," I said sadly. "She is wise and beautiful and has never understood a single strange thing."

"I admire her," the unicorn said. "She must be happy."

"Now," I agreed.

From a marsupial-like pouch at his waist, using both front hooves to clasp it, the unicorn produced a small wooden chess board with crudely carved black and gray pieces.

"Would you care to play?" he asked me.

"Would it be a meaningful game?" I asked back.

He laughed. "There is no meaning in chess that cannot already be found in a green tent amid the wild flowers of Wyoming."

While I considered his offer and his words, the unicorn nudged the board toward me.

"I have no hands," he said. "You will have to do that thing with the pawns so we can decide who moves first."

Obligingly, I 'did the thing with the pawns.'

The unicorn made his choice. And lost.

HIS EYES WERE DUST

In the Ship's mirrored skin he saw his eyes—like dust; his mouth was a white-veiled door opening down to a sunless sea. And he knew himself dead there. And he knew it was a lie, such a lie as a Koora might tell.

Lids went shut against the vision and he turned aside, the movement loud with anger that even here, in the sacrosanct of mother station, Koora thoughts could penetrate. But if it were an enemy saboteur and not just the finger of his imagination, then others would have to find it. He had his own duties to attend. The Ship awaited. His Ship. The most advanced ever produced by the human race.

The Ship read him from the heat and breath that he spilled, and, knowing him, opened like a lover. He slid easily into the web of the pilot's chair, felt it stiffen to support his head and back. The door locked down and the interior of the Ship bloomed in colors of amber, red, and green. The engines thrummed like bees to blush heat up through metal skin and pump ion blood in metal veins.

A hatch opened over the man's head and the helmet descended. He took it with both hands and put it on, feeling the cool mist of anesthesia that numbed his bare scalp to the needles that followed. More screens came alive then, dancing with beta rhythms, and he closed his eyes until he sensed the synchrony of alpha and hippocampal theta building up in the limbic system and riding outward. His death image was gone, to be replaced by stars.

With eyes still closed he stretched out his hands to the open membranes that guided the Ship's limbs, felt them close around his flesh with the faintest of pricks. His legs, bare at hip and thigh, lay against mouths full of electrode teeth that bit ever so gently. He felt once again, in more than orgasmic intensity, of being alive, with metal wings and with eyes that saw in shades of heat across a million miles.

The words of command came into his brain, traveling along a mixture of wire and white matter pathways, and he turned the commands into images and passed them to the Ship. That had been the toughest part of learning to fly, translating verbal language into visual. But he had mastered it well and the Ship was his. As he was hers.

Engine song coursed up an octave. Night eyes watched bay doors open, and he lifted a hand. Following that movement they went out from mother station into space. He turned his head, the Ship with him, and locked thoughts on a distant sun off in the blackness. He drew a breath and let it out.

And they went across night, stabbed like meteor flame through the great silence that sucked up the sound of the engines. There was no sense of movement, the only friction being that of a stray atom or two that bounced like BBs off his alloyed hide. The endorphins could handle that small pain, and there was neuronal blocking to handle the greater when they at last reached the Horsehead Nebula and passed through its scattered glowing dust. With the pain gone it was like listening to the rain as it fell in the great bio-machine gardens beneath his city.

Beyond the Nebula glittered the Pleiades, and past those hot blue suns were other stars that beckoned. Among the latter flickered a tiny drop of light, innocuous as one child in a city of billions. It was there that the man and the Ship were headed.

They came in toward that sun past the cold corpses of the rocky outer worlds, heading for the swirling hells in the land of giants. It was a moon they sought, and found, a yellow disk cratered like the faces of pox children that the man had once seen on a history disk. A mole grew on one cheek of that planetoid face, an ugly thing of irregular design that spread out over the scarred surface like a fungus. It was an outpost of the Koora—vicious, warlike, telepathic, vampiric.

Once, the Koora had been Human, until they came to the long isolation of a planet known as Shimmer. Genetic manipulations meant to allow people to dwell comfortable on the surface of the planet had gone awry. DNA plagues followed as chromosomes snapped and twisted. Deaths and mutations grew geometrically.

Mutations rarely produce entirely new species, but they had produced the Koora. And no true Human could stand the touch of such things, not the foulness of their mind speech and their mind-and-body sex, not the disgust that came when you knew they fed like vampires on the gore of animals. Far better was the purity of the machine and the nourishment of the amino acid vats.

The instinctive hatred Humans felt for the Koora had turned into war within a month after contact was reestablished between the two races. It had become a war of extermination, and to win it Humans had developed the Ship and trained the man. Superior technology could not be countered for long. It never had been before. The destruction of the moon base below would demonstrate that rule once more.

Yet, however much the man wanted to see the vampires dead, he knew they were dangerous fighters and was ready when the first questing tendrils of Koora minds caressed him. Within moments of that touch, silver horrors lifted up from the moon's surface and gusted his way. They came screaming at him, howling banshees and burning phantoms, goblin riders on dragon steeds, all images drawn from the superstitious youth of humankind. The early battles with the Koora had been lost to just such images, but this man knew them for what they were and was unafraid.

He turned as if to flee, the dancing of mental fingers in his head making his flesh crawl and the Ship ripple as his distracted mind caused the engines to vary their thrust. With an effort, he forced his thoughts back into their disciplined channels and let the Ship run, like a stag before hounds.

The Koora patrol came on, casting aside mirage to give open chase, arming their own ships' weapons for the kill. Pimple flashes licked up the man's ion trail. He shut off his exhaust, twisted his head, and went down and right in a hard curve that was only a thousand miles across. Behind him, a wall of yellow flame was built in an instant as the missiles found the end of his exhaust and ignited fusion reactions in their miniature acceleration chambers.

The man and his Ship went to stealth. The Ship cast its own mirages and followed those holographic images in amid the drifting debris of an aborted planet. At the same time, microcircuits in the man's helmet triggered an extremely localized phase shift that blocked the quantum fluctuations the Koora needed to detect someone's emotions and thoughts.

Both man and Ship became a blank to their enemies. Then, together, they began to hunt. It wasn't necessary. With the phase-induced mind block and his advanced technology, the man could have evaded the Koora ships and their primitive sensors indefinitely. But he didn't want to. There were talons nestled under his belly that ached to be used.

Muscles steadied as a hypodermic opened a vein in his leg and gave him adrenaline. Implanted pipettes fed neuroactive peptides and stimulants into target sites in the brain, sending the readouts on his display panel into a frenzy. His mouth went dry and a white light exploded into clarity in his head

With the drugs riding him and the Ship under his hands, the man felt like a god—a vengeful god—and he caught the Koora destroyers one by one, targeting them with signature scopes that read every nuance of their engines and programmed a missile accordingly. He even began to appreciate Koora telepathy. They might no longer be able to detect *him*, but he could still feel them just as they died, their minds going from on to off like a champagne cork coming out. What he liked most about that was how one Koora's death brought others running straight into his weapons.

When the last ship of the enemy patrol was gone, the man signed the stamp of his own engines to a manufactured volcano of destruction on the largest asteroid in the vicinity. He slipped the mark of a few alien torpedoes in as well, hoping the Koora sensors would spot them and think him dead with his last victim. Then he waited, like ice waiting to melt.

The enemy came, and they looked hard, but they didn't find him. The Ship picked off and nullified the more mundane of the sensor beams, and the man's quantum phase block let him escape the far more efficient mind searchers. Even so, his skin was crawling and jumping before the ghostly Koora thoughts that had touched him went away satisfied. Exhausted, he slept.

While the man rested, the Ship served as his womb, an intelligent womb, one that could feed him, and quench his thirst, and carry his wastes away—one that could dream with him in the long night. Though, of course, the dreams had to be gated away from the Ship's muscles. Sleepwalking was not a good idea in a machine that obeyed every image projected.

After a while the man awoke, refreshed, and knew it was time. Ship's sensors told him that space was empty around him and it seemed as if the Koora had bought into his subterfuge and believed him dead. Now he was inside their defense net where they would have no warning of his presence until he was over them. He smiled, and the Ship gathered its legs. He tongued his teeth and it leaped.

They went in flashing, one long sliver of night arrow, and they found the sky above the Koora base empty except for a few armed satellites. The man crooked a finger and the satellites were expanding gas where his scourge missiles had eaten them before their lasers could track.

Koora minds started to stir below him, but they were far too late. The man and the Ship were already over the city by then, screaming in through the faintly thicker atmosphere near the moon's surface. And he clenched his fists. Out of his belly the talons ripped, sliding yellow in the black sky until they mated with ground. The city rippled like a sand castle struck by the fist of a child, and a monstrous flower bloomed upward and outward with petals brighter and hotter than the sun.

Mission over, the man took the Ship up, peeling away the sky like the layers of an onion until in an instant they walked upside down on the shadow of the universe. *Now home*, he had time to think, though he was never to reach that place of imagined safety.

The man had never considered—perhaps no Human could— what the death cry of half a million minds screaming would be like. To feel one Koora death had been a pleasure, to feel half a million was more than agony. And there were not enough endorphins and neuronal blocks in the whole galaxy to stop that much pain. Suit integrity intact, the man died, insane before he went. The Ship lived only a little while longer, never to understand why it felt such emptiness.

* * * * * * *

A hundred years later, long after the war was over, the drifting Ship was found, its engines long since dead and its alloy shell punctured repeatedly by micrometeorites. The man was coiled into his harness like a fetus, electrodes still in his brain, pipettes pumping nothing but void. His mouth, open to scream, was laced with a white webbing of frozen vapor. His eyes were dust.

The Koora turned the Ship into scrap. The man they put into a museum for their children to marvel at. After all, none of them had ever seen a Human before.

INNOCENT LITTLE SIN

She danced
in a mirror of silk and mire,
a death's head lover,
a jackbooted saint.

Followed her home
like a wolf with hungry teeth.
She purred like a blade,
a neon nightmare.

Kissed her mouth,
spanked her cherry heart,
let her tattoo my tongue
with black nails.

Innocent little sin,
till the leather began to weep,
till she reached inside,
showed me her love,

like day-old bruises.

IN TORTURED FLESH

in
tortured
flesh
my
name
she
scrawls

BORDER

At the border of light and rain,
where hell lies suspended
and heaven cracks wide with scorpions,
there rest the gods of desire,
in witch dreams of beauty,
painted like whores with beast mouths,
lying innocent in nameless filth
with roses red as hearts.
Do you know the death they eat?
Do you weigh the poetry of their fuck,
the sick acid white stench
of what they swallow?
At the border of worship and hate
waits the woman I sweat with,
dressed in the music of machines,
carrying the disease of my love.
I saw her eyes flash in wings.
I saw her mind like a shotgun
wedded to the bliss in the teeth
of black-antlered carnivores.
Do you know that I love her?
Or do you scream for her chains
as you slide in the dark wet soul
of her oblivion?

IN MEMORY OF THE SUN

First Prologue

A few strokes of the brush added a little color to the alabaster face that peered out at him from the canvas. A few more slashed the image of silver thorns through the soot-dark hair. His thoughts were yesterdays away.

Where are they now?

One smudge of charcoal below each painted eye, and he had the shadows he wanted there. He deepened them with tempera, and the pigment over dust left a spider web of cracks that seemed to bleed up into the whites of the ikon's eyes. It was an effect that he liked. But his thoughts were tripping down crimson stairs toward another century.

Where are they now?

A finger blotted lips that glistened with too much red, and then he used the finger against the painting in front of him, scoring the line of a fresh wound into the ascetic features that accused him of crimes he had never committed. But wished he had. His mind centered and drew a moment out of the gyre of time.

Where are they now?

He closed his eyes and knew. They were dust—Raevis Valera, who had been his lover and who had died beneath the waves, his bastard teeth in someone else's throat; Jhana Cathay, who had danced a berserk chorea as the phosphor flames leapt up her thighs to her breasts in vain search of a soul to sear;

Sinnea Cathay, who had been...staked.

One long nail, mushroom white, eviscerated the painting from top to bottom and smashed it aside. There were things in it that he had not drawn anyway.

I.

Often of late, in the chalice depths of his wine, he would see an old man's face, a vision that flickered on and off like a lightning stroke. He knew it for what it was, a periodic reminder that his glamour was eroding with the years. And as time passed he was finding it harder and harder to kill that face, with wine, or with blood. He was finding it harder to be sure whether he even wanted to kill it or not, reflecting as it did what he had truly become.

Sometimes, he would look at his hands and see there the liver spots and wrinkles that should have been his lot, as if the fresh flesh that lay across his bones was only a kind of thin glove that had worn through in places. At such times, the cold red tears would overwhelm his eyes, and the red-eyed hunger would overwhelm his thoughts, and he would hunt in the darkness until he had filled some kind of void.

It was surely a blessing that he never remembered the prey he took on such hunts. There would be only snatches, hypnogogic hallucinations, like randomly chosen frames from a fast-forwarded film. He might see the open drainage of a throat, the strip-mined length of a chest, the spackling of serum on his clothing. But he would feel, when he awoke at last from the blood-drunk, as if he had just dropped something infinitely precious into the mud. Such viciousness had never been his way. Valera had occasionally succumbed to it. Jhana had given in to the urge more often than he would have liked. But he and Sinnea had never been...cruel.

It was in the lucid moments following violence that he realized how far he had fallen, that he realized he was aging, and perhaps growing senile. He had thought his kind lived forever, at least as long as they avoided running water, and fire, and stakes, and the sun. But now he knew that something was killing him. He wondered if it was some rare disease Valera had never told him about, or maybe he was just not completely one of the undead. Valera had occasionally taunted him with such, hinting that the bite had not taken as strongly with him as it had with Jhana and Sinnea. For whatever reason, he was aging swiftly, soon to be indistinguishable from the drooling human old that surrounded him. Strangely, he did not find the thought repulsive.

What he did find repulsive was the boredom. He seldom slept much anymore and the hours could not be passed easily. Reading had long since lost its luster, and wine, which he had ofttimes used as a surrogate for blood, held no more release for him. Even his painting passed only a few of the slow crawling moments.

Two hundred years ago his drawings had been greatly in demand, so much demand that the gold they brought in had, when invested wisely, assured him of living well for the remainder of his life, no matter how long that life might be. A hundred years ago he had quit painting, when Sinnea died. He had produced only portraits since that day, three of them. They hung in the hall outside his room, and more than a dozen times during the past few years he'd tried to add a fourth. He had not succeeded.

When the painting failed him, he danced, pirouetting through the empty ballrooms of the huge house, alone and yet not alone. With his mind open he could feel Sinnea and Jhana, and Valera, dancing with him. He twirled and twirled, spinning more and more madly, hands flung out like streamers as his body began to remember, and to change. In one shadow he was himself, in the next he was a woman. In one movement he was human, in the next a monster.

Hair silkened and lengthened down across his spine, then grew coarse and ragged, dreadlocked with gore. His voice, chanting, rose by octaves before dropping again into echoes. He twirled and twirled, faster and faster, now with his palms clasping his breasts, now with himself hard and proud with blood, now with his fingers pressing into the electric dampness between his legs—the teeth in his mouth needling into spires and then blunting back into his gums—now with the sweat sheening his body, and the lace of his shirt wet, and his legs weak. He screamed.

And it was at that moment when the memories always came—Valera, with those harpsichord-player's fingers locked in his hair, Jhana and Sinnea, winged, praising the moon as they glissandoed across each other's skin. There were wet tongues and laughter, and the willingness of the prey. He could recall them watching and waiting in their white silk, a delicious mix of terror and lust on their faces, each one wanting to be the first, each one wanting to bleed into the waiting mouths of their lovers. And oh the fluids were sweet. It wasn't anything like the solitude of these last hundred years. But it *was* a little like the pain of dying.

His dance ever ended in collapse, and in dirge. He had begun to wish that he were dust.

Second Prologue

For a moment he forgot what he was. He stood on the screened balcony of his house, eyes closed as the darkness began to pearl into dawn, and he did not turn away, as if the morning were meant for such as he. The faint gray light that ached on his eyelids began to trigger pain, and with the pain came childhood. It had been long since he revisited it.

He remembered a blond youth running down long rows of standing corn, the leaves turning brown on the stalks and the ripened ears hanging down heavy in their sheaths. Even when he opened his eyes he could still see the overlain images of those days. He could smell the dust and silk of the corn, and feel the weight of the sun on his shoulders, hot and sweetly pleasant through the linen of his shirt. How had he forgotten the sun, he wondered?

But then came a memory of giggling voices and he turned, seeing again his two sisters, hearing again the fake squeals of fear they let out when he jumped through the corn rows at them. And he could hear again, also, the gasps of stronger emotion as they all saw a face appear in the penumbra of a scudding dark cloud that bespoke a sudden storm's approach.

They were to remember that face later, on the night of the fire that took their parents' lives, the night the rider came. The storm's face and the rider's face were the same. Jhana was first to go to the stranger, but Sinnea and he followed after a bit. Raevis Valera had wanted children of his own. So he took them.

Gradually, the pain of the sun became too strong for the memories, and thoughts of childhood faded. He turned away from the balcony when his hair began to smolder.

II.

Once again, in the quiet womb of the hallway, he studied the portraits of his sisters, as well as that of Raevis Valera. In the glow of the oil lamps they were all young and beautiful, and full of lies. He wanted so much to hang his own visage beside the others, but it had to be a true visage, not a virtual one. And each time he tried to paint it he failed. His fingers failed. But then, he'd not had his childhood memories to rely on before, and maybe now his fingers would find themselves again.

Purposefully, he strode to his workroom and set up a pale swatch of canvas. He drew his paints and brushes to him and began to work. And the rhythm was there, down to the dance of knuckles and the click of white nails. Time and thought went away from him. Hunger cried in its bed and was ignored. He moved into the painting, hands pounding and driving, and his flesh was dreaming flesh, and his tongue a brush full of pigment.

When it was finished he knew he had captured his piece.

In the painting he saw an old, old man with cancerous skin and threads of hair, but the eyes were a child's eyes, a blond child's eyes that held no pain. Reflected in the pupils was a clear image of the sun. It was exactly the portrait he'd been seeking, and he went and hung it in the hallway beside the other three.

Gazing at the canvas and seeing those eyes reminded him of something he had not thought of in a long time, and he went and gathered it out of the ancient iron-bound trunk that had been with him for centuries. It was a doll, put together by his father out of corn husks and silk and cob, and it was greased with long handling but still largely intact. The doll had belonged to his sisters, first one and then the other, and now it belonged to him. He held it to his face and smelled the dust, the husks warm against his cheek. He stroked it, in memory of his sisters and of the good earth that had given them life, in memory of the sun that had filled them with beauty. And if he could not have his sisters again, then he damn well could have the sun one last time.

Hanging the doll on a chain around his neck, he drifted up the worn mahogany stairs to the attic, and from there through a window to the roof. The day had passed while he was at his painting, and most of the night as well. But he did not wait for the sun to rise. He changed, unfolding like a sail in a stiff breeze, and the slippage from one skin to another was flawless. Sometimes of late the transformations had failed to go smoothly, and he would end up with a trailing wing or a flat sternum, or bones that were not hollow. But this time he was perfect, better than he had ever been.

The wind was in his wings like in the rigging of a ship, and it took him off the roof into the air. He caught at that air with a long stroke of limbs and pushed it down beneath him, and then another stroke sent him arrowing swiftly upward in the darkness toward the place where the sun already lived. It had been six hundred years since he'd last seen that orb.

The earth had cooled so much in the night that there were

no thermals to ride, and he coursed upward on the strength of his muscles alone. But they did not tire. Above him were the cold sky rivers and the clouds like bleached bones, and above the rivers and the clouds was the rising sun. He spiraled into its light without warning.

For one moment there was no sensation except glorious warmth, and he realized suddenly how cold he had been for the last six centuries. Then the scarlet wound of the sun hemorrhaged over the horizon below him and his tissues caught fire, blooming and bursting. He spun and twisted in agony but did not dive back toward the darkness below. Instead, he climbed higher, his mind wrapped coolly inside his skull for just a moment longer, until the solar corona burst forth around the sun in dazzling rings of jewel-bright color. At that instant even his brain began to burn, and his wings lost their will and left him to fall.

It was a very long way to drop, and the sun had come swiftly and was upon him all the way down to Earth, even as he passed through the clouds and into a thin morning shower that trailed gray vestments through the radiant air. He felt neither the sun nor the rain. He felt only as if he were being cleansed.

Below him in the fields there ran a father and a son, both racing for shelter and both looking up at the raindrops that struck on their faces and tongues. Only the father saw the shape of a young blond child that seemed to dissolve in the air above his head. Only the father saw the nimbus of a glory that appeared around that shape.

But it was the son who found the corn-husk doll at the place where it had fallen upon the ground.

ABOUT THE STORIES

The Cold of Snow and Ghosts: This is the first story I wrote about the vampire Kainja. Completed in 1992, it was published in 1993 in *Prisoners of the Night*. (Later, I used this same name for a very different kind of character when I got lost for a few years in the world of chat. That's a story I'm not yet ready to tell. Maybe when everyone from that insane time is dead.)

Wanting the Mouth of a Lover: This is the second Kainja story, and reveals that Kainja is Judas Iscariot. (I loved this title and later used it for my chapbook of vampire haiku, published by *Spec House of Poetry* in 2008.) The story was written in 1993 and published in *Prisoners of the Night* in 1994. *POTN* was very good to me. Thanks, Alayne!

Vessel for the Holy: The third Kainja story. I postulated that Jesus could be cloned from Judas Iscariot's blood, who drank from the cup of *Jesus'* blood at the Last Supper. Some folks find this blasphemous; I actually think it honors the Christian tradition. It certainly says that Jesus truly was God. Written in 1995, published in 1997, also in *Prisoners of the Night*. I much enjoyed writing the Kainja stories, though they were tough to do, and I have another in the series that's about a third done. It'll be the last, but I couldn't tell you when it might be finished.

Clowns in the Dark: Written in 1986, published in 1990. It was the first story I sent to the highly respected vampire anthology series called *Prisoners of the Night*, and I was happy but a bit surprised when they took it. It started a long relationship with the editor, Alayne Gelfand. The plot is not that strong so maybe the dark, surrealistic writing sold it. I still like this story, and its title.

Messiah: This was the first and is still one of the few stories I've written directly for a specific market. I saw an ad in *Writer's Digest* in 1989 for *Dead of Night* magazine, which wanted vampire stories under 1000 words. I immediately wrote "Messiah." The original title was "Dracula Messiah," but the editor, Lin Stein, thought the "Dracula" revealed too much. I agreed and much prefer the shorter title.

This is the third story I sold, the second one to be published, and the first that I got a check for ($10). That was in 1990. The influence here is clearly from my Catholic upbringing. Again, some people call this story blasphemous. I can't see it. A vampire—an evil creature—is healed by the blood of Jesus. Wouldn't that make Jesus a pretty special person?

The end here is changed from the original, by the way. The last four lines of the 1990 version read:

"No," she said. "I do not understand."

"Only because you do not know what I am," he said. "Or what I was."

"And what was that?" she asked.

He smiled, and she saw the long teeth in his mouth and grew afraid.

Night Fall: A few years after "Messiah," I wrote another vampire tale for *Dead of Night*. The story occurs in the time it takes two people to jump out of an airplane and parachute to earth. They land a little differently than they started. Published in 1994.

Love in the Time of Cyber Sex: Written in July/August 2003 for an anthology to be entitled "Erotic Women," which was never published. It sees print here for the first time. This is the closest I've ever come to revealing the agony and glory of the years I spent on the Chat. To those days, and to those friends and intimates from *The Gathering* who still remember, I offer you thanks and blood. To the ones who weren't my friends, well, you know what I offer you.

The Poetry of Blood: The first couple of paragraphs were written long ago. I finished the story in 2010 for this collection.

What Was Asked; What Was Given: I haven't written many stories with female protagonists. This is one. I've generally avoided female leads because I don't want to get it wrong; I don't want to just write a male character in a female body, which is a criticism leveled at genre fiction on occasion. But Tanquil became very real to me and I had to tell her story.

First written as a straight heroic fantasy in 1993, it lacked something and I soon rewrote it as it appeared in *Prisoners of the Night* in 1995. Later, I revised the heroic fantasy version and it sold too, in 2002, to Tom and Virginia Johnson at *Classic Pulp Fiction Stories.*

When the White Mist: Written in 2000 for a friend and originally called "Dappled in the Fog." I wasn't sure where to send it and tried some contests without any luck. But I continued to believe in the writing and in 2007 it found a good home with Barbara Custer at *Night to Dawn.*

Thorn: I like to think that, with an exception or two, my vampires are not stereotypical. The vamps in this tale are roses. This was the first vampire story I wrote (1986), and my second horror story to be published (1989). It won 8th place in a contest—now *that's* a contest for new writers—and appeared in the resulting anthology, *Tales on the Twisted Side*, under its original title, "Roses and Thorns." Thanks to those who worked at Skye Isle Enterprises, especially Ann Wilmer-Lasky, the publisher. The piece has been substantially revised for this collection.

The Lady Wore Black: I love good titles—my favorite being Harlan Ellison's "I Have No Mouth and I Must Scream"—and I consider them important pieces of a story. That's why I don't include my name after titles on submissions. The title is part of the story. My name isn't. I enjoy thinking up titles and almost never borrow one. "The Lady Wore Black" is an exception. The line comes from a Queensryche song. That song's music inspired the tale, although my story has nothing to do with the song other than that line. I used "The Lady Wore Black" merely as a working title for the story but never found anything that fit better. Written in 1986, it was extensively revised in 1992 before being published in *Prisoners of the Night*.

Rorschach God: Written in October 2009 on a laptop as I sat on my deck and watched the birds and the woods. I'd been thinking that I'd gotten stale in my writing and wanted to break out of that rut with something weird. This came out, and in slightly different form—under the title "Lost in Greenery"—it won me a plush Chtulhu from the wonderful writer and blogger D. Lynn Frazier. This is the piece's first print publication.

River Road; Night Music: This story was written for a specific anthology called *Erotic New Orleans*, which was edited by the talented Debb De Noux and published in 2001. No vamps or werewolves here, but something akin to a ghost. Though there are horror elements in the piece, I really think it's much more of a love story, the first one I ever wrote.

Heaven: In 2008, on my blog, I ran a series of flash fiction stories for Halloween. I thought some of them came out pretty well, including this one. The ending has been revised.

Hunger: Another flash fiction, originally written to a prompt from blog friend and talented writer Bernita Harris. I liked how it turned out and used it in my 2008 Halloween blog series before revising it again for its first print appearance here.

Shadow Dream: This was the second story I ever wrote that I thought publishable. The first was "Death Turned Away," which is not in this collection. Both were written in 1984-1985, while I was in graduate school. These stories show how my writing has always run in two streams, one in horror, the other in fantasy. "Death" was horror; "Shadow Dream" is fantasy.

"Shadow Dream's" plot is cliché, of course. A man discovers at story's end that he's been dead all along. Maybe every new writer pens such a tale. But, while the idea is old, I'm still proud of the prose. It's very surrealistic, a quality that marked much of my early writing.

In 1990, "Shadow Dream" finished 3rd in a contest and paid

me $20, some of the first money I ever made writing. ("Death" finished 1st in a different contest.) It was published in Ralph E. Vaughan's delightful magazine, *Sozoryoku*, in 1991, and has been reprinted several times. The idea came out of nowhere. In those days, I usually thought up a title that triggered my imagination and then just started typing. Things…developed. Not very "writerly," but it's how things worked for me. Many of my short pieces are still written this way.

Shadow Wine: A sequel to "Shadow Dream," meant to be the second in a series that never materialized. Written in 1985, it was never submitted because I wasn't happy with it as a stand-alone story. I changed the ending and revised the piece substantially for this book, although I tried to maintain the surreal style that marked its prequel. It *still* feels a bit unfinished to me.

Goodies: Written in July of 2004 after I was invited to contribute to an anthology called *Small Bites*, which was put together by Garrett Peck and Keith Gouveia to raise money to help with Charles Grant's medical bills. Since I always enjoyed Charles's work, I was happy to do it. Submissions were limited to 500 words. Mine was a kind of Little Red Riding Hood meets Werewolves and Zombies story. I owe the title to a friend of mine, David Lanoue.

Lily White and Red: The opening two paragraphs of this piece were written years ago. I turned that opening into a story for this collection.

In the Shadow of the Rose: My favorite subgenre in fantasy is "heroic" fantasy. "Shadow of the Rose" fits that category more clearly than "Shadow Dream" and "Shadow Wine." It was also written in 1985. Perhaps you can see that I was in love with the word "shadow" in those days. I also tended toward very simple plots, such as this one in which light equals evil instead of good, and dark equals good instead of evil. Wow! Aren't you amazed?

Still, I rather like the writing here, and I like the main character—Jaal Harkest. I once thought I'd write more stories about him, but that never happened. The story placed 4th in the same contest as "Shadow Dream" and was later published by *Sozoryoku* in 1992. It has been revised for this book.

Lovers: Written in 1990 and published that year in C. Michael Muller's *Nightscript*, which I believe put out only one issue. "Lovers" was the first story I ever tried to write "fast," and isn't that what "real" writers do? It was completed in about two hours, but by now it's been tweaked a hundred times. This is also the first story I wrote using an idea generating method called RQW3R, which is described in *Write With Fire*, my book on writing. It involves asking and answering a series of questions that help generate scenes. I no longer use this method *consciously*, but I believe that's because it's become second nature.

I Am Here: Written in 1997 for a friend who was feeling very lonely and depressed. The ending was virtually the same as published here, but without the last line. My friend told me the story helped and I was glad to hear it. Then came this anthology, and I just had to twist the sweet ending around to something a little different.

Cold Where Your Love Lies: First written in 1995, this seemed unfinished to me and was never submitted. Sometimes it takes a long time to work through a story. It wasn't until I started putting this collection together that I saw how to end the piece. It has not been previously published.

Thief of Eyes: Written in 2001 for a theme anthology. That project never got funded so I removed the theme elements and sent it elsewhere. It scored the opening slot in *The Parasitorium: Terrors Within*, a 2004 horror anthology put together by my good friend Del Stone, Jr. The story got honorable mention in the 2005 *Year's Best Fantasy and Horror*, and was reissued in 2009 as an audio podcast by *Fear on Demand* (fearondemand.wordpress.com/). In an odd twist, the editor for *Fear on Demand* is Sidney Williams, whose invitation to that 2001 theme anthology is the reason the tale exists. Nine years later, Sid finally got to publish it. I'm rather proud of the opening: "She had the lips that Satan dreamed of in his long fall to Hell."

Hunter's Moon: This was originally entitled "Once and Future Wolf," but that title gave away too much. Written as a flash piece in 2004, it was revised and expanded in 2009 for David Cranmer's *Beat to a Pulp*. Amazing how long it can be between a story's genesis and its completion.

Night Raptures: I wrote this in grad school but didn't like the original ending and never submitted it. Then, in 2005 I read about a contest for *Descending Darkness* magazine. I realized I could put a nice twist on the story's ending and it won first place in the contest, earned me $75 bucks Canadian and some prizes, and was published. I guess the lesson is, never give up on those old stories.

Prince of the Dark Trail: I'm not exactly sure when this was written, in the late 1990s or early 2000s, I think, but I remember perfectly who it was written for. This entire book is dedicated to her, and that's why it's here. The ending has been changed from the original to reflect the fact that she's now my wife. The piece has not been previously published.

Unicorn Lost: This story may seem out of place in this collection but I'm rather fond of it and I suppose Unicorns are no less fantastic than vampires and werewolves. I don't really believe in the "muse" who strikes from on high, but sometimes stories sure arrive from realms unknown. This piece arrived in 2001. It's more literary and open ended than my typical stuff. I submitted it to a bunch of literary magazines without any luck and largely gave up on it. Then, in 2008, I saw a call for unusual stories about dragons. I revised the story accordingly and it sold to *Dragons Composed*. The Unicorn version appears here for the first time.

His Eyes Were Dust: Written very early in my career (1986), this story finally found a home in 1995 in *Technomancer*, an early online magazine. It has been revised for this printing. I think you can see the influence of Ray Bradbury in the prose.

In Memory of the Sun: Written in 1990, this story was rejected initially because the vampire was too stereotypical. He is, but that was really my intention; I wanted to write about a vampire confronting encroaching senility. Margaret L. Carter published the piece in 1991 at *The Vampire's Crypt*. I'm still pretty fond of it.

ABOUT THE POEMS

Proverbs: Written in 1998. Published in Michael Pendragon's *Penny Dreadful* in 2001.

Judas Nailed his Mouth Open: This poem led directly to the Kainja vampire stories. Written in 1992, it was published in 1995 in *Once Upon a Midnight*, a collection edited by Jame Riley, Michael Langford, and Thomas Fuller. The poem received honorable mention in *1996's Year's Best Fantasy and Horror*.

Holocaust in Rosary: Written in 1994, also appeared in *Once Upon a Midnight*. This was originally going to be the title for the whole anthology but the word "holocaust" is just too loaded, I think.

Twisted Little Thing: Written in 1997, published in *Penny Dreadful* in 1999. Back when I hung out on "The Gathering Chat," we often wrote spontaneous poems back and forth on the wall. This is one of many I wrote at that time, quite a few of which have since seen print.

Wet Acid Angel: Another "Chat" poem. Written in 1998, published in *Penny Dreadful* in 2000.

Flagellated: This one went through a lot of submissions before finally appearing on Brutal Dreamer's website. Despite its history, I like it and think it fits this collection. Written in 1996, finally published online in 2003.

Loud Love: Written 1998, published online by *Blood Moon Zine* in 2000. The title is borrowed from the *Soundgarden* song of that name, although the poem has nothing in common with the song.

Moth: Written in 2000, published online in 2003 by *Gothic Revue*

Soft: Written in 1995, published in *Penny Dreadful* in 2002.

Fragments: Written in 2003, it appears for the first time here.

Cold Blood: Written in 1991, published in Gary William Crawford's *Night Songs* in 1994.

Maps: Written in 1995, published in *Penny Dreadful* in 2000.

Forgiven: Written in 1991 while I was half drunk and pissed off at my first wife. It was published in *Star*Line* in 1994, when Marge Simon was editing it. It was nominated for the Rhysling Award but didn't win. It truly *is* an honor just to be nominated for that award, though.

Dead to Write: Written in 1994 and published in Meg Thompson's *Rouge et Noir* in 1995.

Death Is: Written in 1999, published in 2000 in *Penny Dreadful*. Some lines from this poem were used in the story "Thief of Eyes."

Blue Soul: Written in 2002 and published in David C. Kopaska-Merkel's *Dreams and Nightmares* in 2008.

Rotted Angels; **Rotted Angels 2**: "Rotted Angels" was written in 1997, "#2" in 2000. "Rotted Angels" was accepted by a magazine but never published—until now—while "Rotted Angels 2" was published in *Star*Line* in 2006 under the title "Rotted Angels." Still with me? *That* "Rotted Angels" received honorable mention in the 2007 *Year's Best Fantasy and Horror*.

License to Bleed: Written in 1995, a different version of this appeared in *Star*Line* in 1996. I think the version here is better. Thanks to my "Inklings" writing group for feedback.

Song to a Rose: I have a tape recorder for my long commute and once in a while a poem occurs to me on my drive. This "commuter" poem occurred in 2007. It appears here first.

Portrait of Her in Darkness: Written 1995, substantially revised for this first printing.

Voodoo Gods: Written in 1997, published online in *Blood Moon Zine* in 2000.

Like a Whisper: Written 2001. This is its first publication. No vampires at all, but in keeping with some of the more romantic elements of this collection.

She's a Killer: This is actually the lyrics to a song I wrote in 1990, which has never been produced. It was published as a poem in *Dumar's Reviews* (thanks Denise) in 1991.

Innocent Little Sin: Written in 1998, during my time on the Chat, and published online in *Blood Moon Zine* in 2000. The first stanza was revised for this book.

Border: Written and published in 2000 in *Hazmat Review*. It remains one of my favorites.

Haiku: The haiku sprinkled throughout appear here for the first time.

ABOUT THE AUTHOR

CHARLES ALLEN GRAMLICH grew up on a farm in Arkansas, near the foothills of the Ozark Mountains, then moved to the New Orleans area in 1986 to teach psychology at a local university. He's since sold four novels, two nonfiction books, and numerous short stories. His tales, while mostly in the genres of horror, science fiction, and fantasy, have also included westerns, children's stories, mainstream fiction, slipstream works, and experimental pieces. Charles has also published poetry and nonfiction, the latter ranging from reference works on science and psychology to articles on writing.

Charles is a member of SFPA (the Science Fiction Poetry Association). He is an editor for *The Dark Man: The Journal of Robert E. Howard Studies*, and currently lives in Abita Springs, Louisiana with his wife Lana. He has one adult son, Joshua. His blog can be found at:

http://charlesgramlich.blogspot.com

www.ingramcontent.com/pod-product-compliance
Lightning Source LLC
Chambersburg PA
CBHW050414260626
47156CB00003B/1005